CITIES OF THE DEAD

Linda Barnes

D1119815

FAWCETT CREST • NEW YORK

A Fawcett Crest Book
Published by Ballantine Books
Copyright © 1986 by Linda Appelblatt Barnes

Library of Congress Catalog Card Number: 85-25155

ISBN 0-449-21188-6

This edition published by arrangement with St. Martin's Press, Inc.

Great restaurants and great chefs abound in New Orleans, but all the characters in this book are fictitious, and any resemblance to actual persons, living or dead, is purely coincidental.

Manufactured in the United States of America

First Ballantine Books Edition: May 1987

A CREOLE CRIME CAPER

Fawcett Crest Books
by Linda Barnes:

BITTER FINISH

BLOOD WILL HAVE BLOOD

CITIES OF THE DEAD

DEAD HEAT

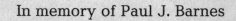
In memory of Paul J. Barnes

Acknowledgments

Lt. Byron L. Anderson, Commander of the Homicide Unit of the New Orleans Police Department, graciously answered my many questions concerning the workings of the Homicide Unit. I would like to thank him for his help.

My Louisiana friends, Craig Braquet, Mike Broussard, Marcy Clerc, and David Landskov, guided me through restaurants and graveyards, and checked the manuscript for accuracy. Their kindness is greatly appreciated.

Steven Appelblatt, Richard Barnes, Susan Linn, James Morrow, and Karen Motylewski commented on the manuscript in various stages of completion. Their suggestions were generously given and gratefully received.

Prologue

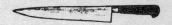

Where can you hide a body in a graveyard?

Saint Louis, Number Three, was a walled city. Closed. Apart. A city of the dead, with brick walls twelve feet high and ten feet thick, built to hold the wall tombs. The old Creoles called them ovens, for their resemblance to bakers' ovens. No one living moved inside those walls at night. That was why they decided to meet there. Total privacy.

The man who was still on his feet groaned and dropped the heavy shovel on the path, in the alley between the tombs. It struck the gravel hard, clanging, and jolted him.

Had anyone heard?

He was wet. His chest, his armpits, his groin, felt unpleasantly damp. He fumbled at the buttons on his checked shirt with shaky fingers, pulled a button off in his hurry, and, cursing quietly, stuffed it into his jeans. The breeze that lifted the Spanish moss in the tall trees bordering the Bayou St. John didn't come into the cemetery to cool or dry him.

The dead man's body had stopped leaking blood from the head wound. Blood dappled the gravel path. The living man knelt, groped the ground at his knees, found his flashlight, and cautiously shone it at the closest tomb, wondering if blood had spattered the marble.

It was one of the older family tombs, one of a row. Some were miniature Greek temples, some were tiny peak-roofed houses. This one was granite, with three steps leading up to a panel bearing many names. A carved marble plaque near the roof gave the family name. *La Famille Hubèry.* A tuft of grass stuck out of a crack in one side of the granite. Two empty urns flanked the steps. No dirt, no flowers. The marble glinted clean and white in the flashlight beam.

Louise Hubèry. 1794–1866. Natif de St. Dizier, décédé le 29 Décembre à l'âge de 72 ans et demi. Chère épouse d'Estephan, mère de . . .

He read the tablet twice. Started over with Louise again. Seventy-two years. More than three times the years of the man at his feet. And Louise Hubèry had died well-loved, with a husband and children to buy the expensive carving on the marble plaque. A family tomb to lie in. Friends to mourn.

Where can you hide a body in a graveyard?

In a tomb.

There had to be an open tomb. There were always burials, almost daily burials here now. The records would be in the archdiocesan office, along with the plot number of the freshly opened tomb, the diagram showing where it was located, which alley, which crossing.

What difference did it make whose name was on the tablet, whether people marched in endless procession to fill vases, light candles, pray? It had made no difference to Louise Hubèry, dying in the fullness of her days a hundred years ago. It would make no difference to the dead man lying at his feet. Nothing would make a difference to him again. Rain would fall. Snow would cover him. Earthquake, fire, storm were all the same to him.

The living man found that his face was wet, too. He couldn't tell if it was sweat or tears.

One

"Tell me about the man who was killed," Spraggue said.

The Orleans Parish lock-up smelled of disinfectant and sweat. A woman sat on the narrow holding-cell bunk, her head cradled in her hands. Staring down at her, Spraggue thought that someone else, anyone else, would have made a spunkier leading lady for a police drama. Dora Levoyer, Aunt Mary's longtime cook, looked small and shrunken, as if she'd been trying to disappear and only partially succeeded.

"I wonder," she said softly, "if I can make you understand." She glanced up and studied his face as if she were committing it to memory.

"Try me."

She used to leave him secret late-night snacks in the refrigerator. Years ago. Strawberry tarts with flaky pastry and chantilly cream. Homemade pâté smeared on crusty fresh-baked bread. If he mentioned her kindness, she'd blush and twist her apron in her hands. Compliments to the chef had to be relayed through the proper channels.

When he'd moved out of the big house, he hadn't missed the family ghosts, the thick Oriental rugs, the Sèvres porcelain, the maid service. But he still dreamed about Dora's cooking.

She took a deep breath and shifted her gaze, focusing on the bare cinderblock wall. Her voice sounded harsh in spite of the French elision that usually made her speech musical. "It is hard for me to talk about it to anyone—and to tell that lawyer, a man I do not know at all, it would be even harder than to tell your aunt, who thinks of me so highly I cannot bear to see the disappointment in her eyes."

"Nobody's disappointed, Dora. Nobody's judging you. Just don't tell me the worst, okay? Don't confess to murder, because I'm no priest, and no doctor, and no lawyer, and I'd have to—"

"Anything I say, you must repeat to those policemen?"

"Well . . ." Spraggue peered around to see where the guard had come to roost. "Not everything," he murmured.

"It seems I have no choice. So listen and don't be unhappy if I cry. I cry too easily and that is another reason I would not have a stranger here. It is so frustrating, such a weakness, to cry in front of strangers—and yet whenever I think—This is difficult for me. It is a business I have not spoken of for fifteen, eighteen years. And if it were not for Denise Michel—"

"Isn't she some kind of chef? Doesn't she write cookbooks?"

"To call Denise a chef is to call a beautiful, perfect silver Rolls-Royce a car. But she makes her living by cooking, yes. And she invited me here to a gathering of chefs, the Great Chefs of New Orleans they call themselves, and she was very insistent. And now I know why."

"Go on, please."

Dora hesitated. "How old do you think I am, *monsieur*?"

"I'm no good at guessing ages," he lied. He would have

4

started at sixty easily, but he seemed to remember Aunt Mary saying that Dora was younger than she looked.

"Never mind. In France, when I was growing up, it was wartime and there were many shortages and, in my case, particularly a shortage of parents, and a shortage of food, and a shortage of care, and so I grow old before my time. But that is not here or there, except that perhaps this new unhappiness will age me still more and . . ."

He wanted to take her hands and comfort her, but her erect spine and sad dignity were hard-won barriers that warned him to keep his distance. Once they crumbled, he might not get the story.

"I'm sorry, *monsieur*, it is even harder than I thought." She drew a ragged breath and started again. "Denise invited me to come, to help her by giving a workshop, and I thought, so, I still have one friend and I should come when she asks me because friends are not so plentiful for me and I have not seen her since I left New Orleans many years ago."

"How many years ago?"

"Mon Dieu! Aidez-moi." She used her French unconsciously and almost smiled when she realized her lapse. "Long ago. I was born in Lyons, where the food is the best. But when I am a young woman, I cannot get work— and my parents are dead—and there are not so many young men—so I come to New Orleans because it has a French name and is very romantic in the tour books. Maybe 1960. I was, perhaps, twenty-six years old."

Ten years younger than he would have guessed. "Go on," he said.

"It's hard to tell an old story. You remember what you were once, and you look at yourself how you are now. And you weep. Not for your looks, but for your dreams."

Even with the frazzled hair and the wrinkles and the baggy, indeterminate-colored dress, when Dora smiled, Spraggue got a glimpse of an odd, shadowy, bone-deep beauty that hadn't entirely disappeared over the years.

"I met a man—how many stories must begin like that—I met a man in New Orleans. I was a sous-chef, an underling to an old man who must have died long ago, in a restaurant that no longer exists—and a man came into the restaurant and he talked to me about food and life and his family and mine. I was lonely and I was looking for someone, that I cannot deny, because I was by then—what—more than thirty years of age and that is an age that sees loneliness as a very long time. And I married this man—and he went away. I tried to find him, yes, but then it seemed to me so shameful that I could not bear it. For my husband, he was not dead, or in an accident, and he must have run off with someone else. Because he was not such a good husband after all. But he was mine. I thought . . . ."

"Go on."

"I thought because I was . . . ."

"Because?"

She shook her head, a vague wistful tremor. "I was deceived. I knew inside me that I would not marry again. I could not support the pain again. And perhaps I knew I would not be asked. I don't know. I moved away from my memories. I went to New York and I worked many places there, and the fact that I was married came in handy, when I needed an excuse, you know, not to become attached to one of the other chefs or to the restaurateur. It was sometimes convenient to be another man's woman because many men do not believe that a woman can live by herself and not be bitter or angry or a rival to them. So I was safe as a married woman and rarely people questioned me about this man and sometimes I said he had died or we were separated. I tired of restaurant work. I went to Boston to cook for your aunt. I never knew what happened to this man I married. I left word with a few friends, with Denise, so that if he should want to reach me, he could. But after so many years, almost twenty years, it was sure that he was dead or happy elsewhere. I did not think about him. You understand?"

He nodded.

"Denise said nothing about this when she invited me. Only that it was an honor for her to be the hostess of this affair and she would be grateful if I would attend as her guest. I have much vacation time coming to me from your aunt and I wrote that I would come."

"How long have you been here?"

"What is today? Thursday? Friday? A night like last night cannot be measured. I have been in this city since Saturday, but I did not realize what had prompted Denise to call for me until Tuesday. Now it seems to me I have been naive, stupid, but it was not until then that I realized why this man, this man Joseph Fontenot, is familiar to me. He is very different, you understand? More than a difference of years. He limps. My Jacques did not limp, nor did he wear those thick spectacles. This man is heavy; he has a stomach, and my Jacques was thin like a reed, a well-made man. This man has a mustache; he is balding. My Jacques was smooth-faced and his hair was curly like a boy's. But something is the same . . . And I know suddenly when I am seated near him at dinner, near Denise also, that he is not Joseph Fontenot, but he is my husband. And I know that this is why Denise has brought me here, although I cannot say from what well her thought sprang up. If she wants to hurt me I do not know why. If she wants to hurt the woman who is now Jacques' wife, I do not know why. But I know now that I had no marriage—"

"You said you married him—"

"Is a marriage legal in this country when one of the parties is already married? For last night, Denise is asking this man, who calls himself Joseph, questions. She and I have already spoken, you understand, when I recognize him, when I realize what is going on. And she says to me, I will ask him these things and you will see what is the truth. And I phone your aunt, beg her to join me. Never would I ask for such a favor, but I am, how do you say, in a quandary. I do not know what to do, what is the legal thing to do so that this man has no right to tell anyone that once I was his wife. And your aunt will know about lawyers and things. So Denise asks questions: How long are you married? And Jeannine, the wife, says, twenty-four years. So he was wedded to her long before he married me. And they have a child, also, a daughter eighteen years, and I would not wish a child to know that her father was the kind of man who would wed two women—"

"Did you ever get a divorce?"

She rubbed the palm of her left hand with her right forefinger, tracing the red marks where her nails had bitten her flesh. "No," she said. "At first I did not want one. And then I did not need one. There was no one else I wished to marry."

She averted her face in a vain effort to keep some privacy. Tears slid down her cheek. Years ago, when he'd been a private investigator, Spragueu had found the forced confidences of strangers painful. The pain of someone you knew was worse. So different from the comfortably fake anguish of actors. Actors blurted dark secrets with relish; that was their function. Real people covered wounds with scar tissue, or hid them till they festered.

"Okay," he said gently. "Tuesday you realized that Joseph Fontenot could be Jacques, your missing husband. You spoke to your friend, Denise, about it. You arranged a questioning session for this banquet last night—"

"Yes." She seemed strong again, recovered. "I asked your aunt particularly to remember the conversation so that later on we could find out the best thing to do, but I did not tell your aunt that the man had married me."

"And after dinner, the man was killed."

"Yes, and, oh, *monsieur*, listen to me closely, I may have hated that man once as I loved him once, but it is all so long ago. I think that it was a different woman entirely who loved and hated so passionately. A better woman perhaps, but not the person I have become. When I sit across from him at the table, he is like a stranger to me. I try to

8

summon up the anger, to feel betrayed, as Denise says I am, but there is nothing, only a deep sadness for what I was and will never be again."

Her voice was flat and bewildered, scarcely louder than a whisper. He knew what a good actress could do with lines like those, and he half believed her just because she hadn't used any of the vocal tricks. He didn't think he knew a liar good enough to serve that up without embellishment, without even a catch in the throat.

"You didn't kill him?"

"Oh, no. I didn't. Believe me. I am not the heroine of Greek tragedy. I am only the cook." Her smile was wry, a touch bitter. "And," she said, "I wish to hire you to prove me innocent."

"I think my aunt has already hired me."

"She has done enough for me. I will hire you myself."

"I'll see what I can do."

"Please." She focused her attention on the gray cinderblocks, as if she were trying, by sheer force of will, to keep herself from seeing something else. She swallowed hard, opened her mouth, closed it without making a sound.

"Anything else I should know?" he asked.

She shook her head, her lips pressed tight.

"You're sure?"

"I've told you everything, *monsieur*. My whole life."

Spraggue just nodded. Nobody ever told you everything.

Two

"**S**he confess?"

The man who trumpeted the question looked like he'd been waiting in the wings to play the role of Southern sheriff. Pushing retirement age, he had the standard paunch, a gentle cloud of whitish hair, round cheeks, and a bulbous nose. His level gray eyes seemed to belong to another face.

Aunt Mary was waiting too. And even Southern sheriff-types deferred to Aunt Mary. Diminutive, elderly, she might be, but she exuded the authority that came with years of command. Underneath the charm, there was steel.

She offered the sheriff a dimpled smile and said, "May I speak to my nephew alone?"

Spraggue said, "Have you got a lawyer for Dora?"

"Of course."

"Well, get him and let the cops in." To the central casting sheriff he said, "Dora's ready to tell you everything she told me."

"That so?" said the fat man. "And just why would 'everything' be so touchy private before and so godawful public now?"

Spraggue shrugged. Any cop ought to know that repetition was less painful after the first time.

The fat cop said, "You can use the lieutenant's office. Hayes, show Miz Hillman and her nephew back there, okay? These hallways get you all turned around."

The office was small. One metal desk sat two feet in front of a window graced with broken matchstick blinds. The window faced out on a brick wall.

Mary stood on tiptoe and planted a kiss on her nephew's cheek. She sat cautiously on the single spindly guest chair and motioned him to a cracked imitation-leather swivel job behind the desk. Her rumpled gray silk suit, pink bow askew—an evening outfit—meant she hadn't slept last night. Her smile erased the fine wrinkles in her skin and made her seem far younger than her seventy-odd years, her vitality more attuned to the red in her curling hair than the silver.

"I'm sorry, Michael," she said. "I hope it wasn't too much trouble for you to get away."

Trouble? Hell, no. No trouble. Just walked out on an Equity acting job. Left the director with a lame excuse and a moron of an understudy. Screwed my reliability rating in every theater in the known world. No trouble.

All he said out loud was "No," and Aunt Mary beamed as if she'd known it all along.

"Quickly now," she said. "What did Dora say?"

"Imagine my surprise to hear you were in New Orleans," Spraggue replied, raising one eyebrow. "I leave you one night, safe and sound in Boston and—"

Mary fluttered her hands. "I know. I know. I should have told you. I apologize abjectly. Things happen. Now what did Dora say?"

"First you're going to tell me what's going on so that I can make some sense of what she said."

"I don't know what's going on," Mary protested. "I feel like someone who's been given one of those terrible, huge jigsaw puzzles to play, except it got all mixed up

11

with another one, and I've got half the giraffe pieces and half the leopard pieces, and they've both got spots, sort of, but they'll never match up."

"Do you want to get some sleep first, Aunt Mary?"

"Oh, darling. No. I don't really. I *am* tired, but I can talk. I'll stop babbling about giraffes and leopards and start at the beginning." She closed her eyes and said, "Maybe this is the onset of senility."

Spraggue said, "Garbage. I pity the police department that tangles with you, lady."

She sat up straighter. "Okay. Report. Hillman to Spraggue. I shall try to be as factual and succinct as possible. If I stray, bear with me."

Spraggue kept a grin off his face with effort. "Shoot."

"Wednesday morning—let me see, it was ten o'clock because the stock exchange had just opened—I got a phone call that Pierce insisted I take. It was Dora, sounding quite odd. She's worked for me for what? eight years now, cooking beautiful food and only complaining when I don't entertain enough, and never getting persnickety about adding more garlic if I like. A gem. Well, in all that time she never asked for a vacation, just took her days off when I traveled. I mean, it must get so dull for her, cooking for an elderly widow, when she used to awe the New York restaurant critics. But she insisted she liked the slow pace after so many years of hullabaloo. I kept urging her to take a trip, put a little excitement in her life, and finally, last week she asked if it would be all right if she went to New Orleans for some cooks' get-together bash and, of course, I was delighted. Pierce and I can get by on our own, although my cooking is dull at best and his is distinctly bizarre. All that curry—"

Spraggue cleared his throat. Mary's cheeks grew pink and she said, "I'm wandering, aren't I? Well, back to basics: Dora's phone call. She asked me—begged me—to come down to New Orleans for a day or two. Now normally that would be out of the question, but there was

12

something in her voice, and, well, when someone has worked for you for eight years and never said a word about her personal life and never asked even a tiny favor—well, I was intrigued. So I came. I said nothing to you because I assumed I'd be back long before our next dinner date with some fascinating tale, instead of being just old stick-in-the-mud me.

"Pierce arranged everything. The airplane. The suite at the Imperial Orleans. I was delighted at the prospect of meeting all those marvelous chefs, tasting their cooking. Dora must have been quite a rising star when she cooked in New Orleans to be included in such select company. Denise Michel—you know, the one who wrote *A Taste of France in New Orleans*—and Paul Armand and Joseph Fontenot—the things that trio does with oysters alone! Well, Dora said she couldn't meet me at the airport because she was helping her friend, Denise, by giving a workshop, something to do with knives, worse luck. But Pierce thought of everything and I had a lovely limo ride to the hotel and got settled in and then there she was.

"Now I expected Dora to be forthcoming in New Orleans. I thought she hadn't wanted to talk about her difficulties on the phone, but would certainly spill the beans in person. Then, when I saw her in the hotel, she clammed up. Said absolutely nothing, except that presently I would understand and I should please be patient. I suspected her of some sort of practical joke. If it had been my birthday, I would have assumed she was in league with you and Pierce to do something drastic, pop me out of a cake, or worse. She invited me to attend the chefs' annual dinner, an awards banquet, that night—Thursday night, you see, I couldn't get out on Wednesday. Too much to finish up—and she said I should dress nicely and the food would be superb and I would be seated at her table and would I please listen closely to the conversation. *Take special note of the conversation*, she said."

Aunt Mary pushed a wayward curl off her forehead. "How detailed do you want me to get?"

"If you're too tired—"

"If I did it for the police, I can do it for you. It's just that I don't know if I'm remembering what happened, or parroting what I told the police. It's all muddled."

Exactly, Spraggue thought. Just what that cop should have known. The first time is always the hardest. The second time, you turn into a bad actor, repeating the words instead of reliving the action.

"Close your eyes," he said gently, "and put yourself back into the time right before the banquet."

"Actor stuff," Mary said suspiciously.

"Yep," Spraggue said. "It works."

"I feel silly. Like I'm pretending to go off into a trance."

"Try it."

Mary pressed her hands against her head. "Michael, it's all whirling and confused—colors and lights and people—"

"You're doing too much at once. Where were you when you first saw Dora on Thursday night?"

"Let me see . . . She knocked on my door, a quiet sort of knock. I was early, already dressed in my gray suit, this one. I remember I had trouble tying the bow, but finally it came out right. I was sitting on the sofa, hoping I wouldn't wrinkle—the suit, that is. I was—"

"Try it in the present tense, Aunt Mary. I *am*—" Spraggue kept his voice low, unobtrusive, an "actor-coaching" voice. He remembered the first director who had used it on him, back in his Royal Academy of Dramatic Art days. After a while it became part of you, a subconscious voice . . . part of you, and separate.

"I *am* reading Lillian Hellman. *Pentimento*. And Dora knocks. I'm expecting the knock. Hoping she'll tell me more about this 'conversation' I'm supposed to note so carefully. I open the door. She looks very nice. No makeup, but a touch of lipstick, which means she considers the occasion as formal as an occasion can be—and she's wearing

14

her beige crepe dress. A very good dress, must have cost a great deal, but not her color at all. Just one of Dora's fade-into-the-background outfits. . . ."

"Does she come in?" The words slipped in easily, prompting, but not breaking the flow of information.

"She says we should start on down. The banquet is in the grand ballroom, on the mezzanine. My suite is on the sixth floor. I remember looking—no, I look into the mirror while we're waiting for the elevator, and Dora's face seems, oh, kind of strained and gray. I put my hand on her shoulder, and, Michael, she clutches my arm, holds it so hard I wince. But then her grip loosens. Still, she keeps her hand on my arm—here—as if I'm her anchor, as if she's a little girl afraid of getting lost in the crowd. . . . And there was—"

"*Is*, Aunt Mary."

"There is a crowd. People streaming up the staircase, all the men wearing dinner jackets, some of the women in long gowns. Flashes of jewelry. Spurts of conversation and laughter. There's a rather unruly mob in front of the doorway. It's not wide enough to accommodate the flow of guests. There's a coat rack filled with coats and I smile because no one in the North would wear a wrap on such a balmy evening."

"Dora, does she speak to anyone?"

"Not a soul. She clings to me, and I say what a beautiful room it is and things like that, to try to put her at ease. It is a lovely room, all gold and ivory, with a pink-and-gold carpet. The chandeliers must have been cleaned the day before. So sparkly and bright. Ten, maybe twelve round tables, and one large rectangular table, raised on a dias. White tablecloths and pointy folded napkins. Cut-glass vases bursting with yellow roses. . . .

"There is an archway into another room, a smaller room hung with banners and signs. The display room. Full of cookware, pots and pans, and food processors and whisks.

15

Knives . . ." Her voice faltered. "I want to look, but Dora pulls me to our table. She's still so quiet."

"How did you know which was your table?"

"Dora knew. It was as though she was taking steps she'd rehearsed before. We were—are—at Table One, which surprises me. Not the big rectangular table, but the one closest to it, on its right. The big table is for the judges and the master of ceremonies. Our table is filled with big shots. Denise Michel herself is there. She's the host of the entire event, and the chef in charge of tonight's meal. A huge woman. Not fat, but tall. Six feet, maybe more. Solid. Strong craggy face, beaky nose. Quick smile. I like her. I like her handshake and her deep voice. She takes over from Dora and introduces me to the others.

"Michael, there's a whole flock of strangers. You know how I hate things like that. I smile and nod and only get them sorted out much later. Four are chefs, five counting Dora. Five chefs. Me. That's six. There are eight at the table. That leaves two more. Oh, you know who was there, sitting right across from me? That food columnist-critic fellow, what's-his-name? You can't turn on the TV without seeing the man. Harris Hampton, that's the name. A disgusting man, really. So smug and superior. Fat and loud and, oh, kind of smarmy. Too genial by half, like some foot-in-the-door encyclopedia salesman. You can tell that no one at the table likes him. And every once in a while he takes this notebook out of his pocket and makes some sort of scribble about the food. Very secretively, you know, like a precocious second-grader guarding his spelling test."

"Who else is at your table?"

"Let me see. Five chefs. Me. The horrible food critic. And there's one spouse, also a chef, but I get the feeling she's not really in the same league as the rest. Jeannine Fontenot. Joseph's wife. Buxom. Dark-eyed. Quite handsome. Wearing very regal burgundy silk. She's quiet, possibly a little shy."

"Tell me about the chefs."

16

"Denise Michel, I've already described. And Dora. Paul Armand. Taller even than Denise. Thin. Very distinguished. Continental manners. You've tasted his food. He owns the Café Creole."

"Mmmmmm."

"Indeed. Then there's Henri Fiorici, from Fiorici's in New York. I don't know if he happened to be in town or if he came down for the dinner. One of those tiny vain men. A popinjay. Scarlet cummerbund and polka-dot bow tie. Very dapper. And so polite. He keeps trying to smooth over all the awkwardnesses—But I'm getting ahead of myself.

"The last chef is Joseph Fontenot. A fat, ugly man. No, I shouldn't say ugly. He's hiding behind a bushy mustache and heavy glasses, and he seems ungainly because he walks with a cane. But he might have been attractive if it weren't for the way he argued. And now when I think of him, I keep seeing him dead."

"Mary, maybe you ought to take a break—"

"Don't treat me like some elderly aunt," she snapped. "We'll just skip any more comment on Joseph Fontenot and I'll go on to the conversation.

"Well, first it's desultory, bursts and silences. Fontenot says something about a funeral, the funeral of an old friend, I think, and that goes over like a brick. No one wants to discuss death over dinner. Someone chimes in with a story about vegetables, how hard it is to get good fresh vegetables anymore. I get the feeling that everyone else knows why we've been chosen to sit together. You know, usually at a big affair, they seat everyone from Peoria together, or everyone who holds office. And after a bit, I decide that all the people at our table, except me, of course, must have been involved in some sort of seminar that afternoon. Because they start an argument, and I get the feeling that it's a continuation of one that's been going on for some time."

"What about?"

"Food processors and knives and graters. It seems a

17

traditional Luddite-versus-Progressive battle to me. And I keep wondering *why* Dora should want me to take special note of whether Joseph Fontenot prefers puréeing through cheesecloth to blending in a Cuisinart—Mr. Fontenot is very vocal in all his opinions and seems to believe he has a direct line to the God-in-Charge-of-Food. Well, I'm keeping track of everyone's rambling, when over the entrée—a trout almondine even murder couldn't make me forget, one of those traditional New Orleans deep-fried trout, perfectly done with a lemony tang—Dora sort of pokes me in the ribs. It's the signal that I should start my careful listening. I'm a bit indignant, having already absorbed all that food processor rigamarole, but I'm also intrigued, so I rev up my concentration.

"Denise Michel starts asking questions. Now Denise is not a social butterfly. She is formidable. Each time a dish comes, she tastes it first, and I get the distinct impression that she disapproves of all this chitchat. It detracts from the food. Which is spectacular. Do you want to hear more about the food?"

"Later. They fed me a sawdust omelette on the airplane."

"Sorry. Denise puts down her fork and knife and begins a formal inquisition. Her target is Joseph Fontenot, although every now and again she'll aim a question at Fontenot's wife. And it's obvious that the whole thing is planned. I mean, the woman has no social graces at all. She doesn't toss these questions into a general flow of wondering how everyone got started in the business. No, she just baldly demands answers. How long have you been married? How long have you lived in New Orleans? Where did you work in 1962? 'Sixty-four? 'Sixty-six? I don't know what to make of it."

"Does Fontenot?"

"I think so." Mary sat very still. "Yes. I think it amuses him."

"And Dora?"

"Keeps getting paler and paler. She's next to me, so I can't see her all the time, but once she squeezes my hand under the table, and her fingers are icy."

"Go on."

"Denise leads him through this catechism and when he's fed up with it, he stands. Doesn't even finish his trout, which Denise takes as an insult. Says something about greeting a friend at another table. Takes off. I'm relieved. I catch Fiorici's eye and I can see he's relieved as well. He smiles and tries to talk to Dora, something about old times in New York. But Dora is practically mute. Denise returns to scrutinizing the salad. A few of the others, *after* they've finished their fish and complimented Denise, take off to socialize, but they all come back quite swiftly. None of us really notice that Fontenot hasn't returned until dessert is served. You've heard of Michel's soufflés? She's made individual raspberry and white chocolate soufflés, and they are spectacular, white and pink like the room, garnished with sprigs of mint. Someone at the head table starts applauding when the trays come out, and Denise blushes brick-red, not at all attractive, you know. And we keep applauding until she stands up. You can tell how pleased she is, even though she's embarrassed. The desserts are served and then we have a problem. You see, our table is polite. We've made a habit of waiting until all eight of us are served to pick up our spoons and forks and dig in. But Joseph Fontenot is not there. Mrs. Fontenot giggles and urges us to go ahead without him. But Denise glowers. So we sit. And it gets quite uncomfortable. And then after a minute or two, Dora bolts. She looks unwell and I ask if she's all right, and she summons up a ghost of a smile and begs me please, not to *déranger* myself. So now we have six squirming diners and eight soufflés that are about to topple.

"Denise gives in, picks up her fork, and we all plunge in with many compliments. The soufflés are marvelous. But Fontenot's is just sitting there, listing to one side—

19

well, it's awkward. And I decide the man ought to come back and eat. Me, the avenging angel. He shouldn't be so rude to his hostess. I didn't realize I had so much of the nursery governess in me.''

Spraggue smiled.

"I excuse myself, saying I want to check on Dora, which isn't exactly a lie. I do go into the ladies' room, but she's gone.''

"Gone?''

"I don't search the stalls. But I call her name and she doesn't answer.''

"Go on.''

"Well, I go into the display room. I don't see Fontenot in the banquet hall, but I could have missed him. People are milling about. The display room seems peaceful and I want a moment to think and, well, I want to see the items on display. So I justify it to myself, saying I'm searching for Fontenot.''

"And?''

Mary's voice dropped to a whisper. "I find him.''

"Be very specific now, Aunt Mary. Tell me what you see and touch and hear and smell . . .''

"The room is dark. The lights must have been on a rheostat and they're turned down low. It's eerie, with all those pots and pans hanging overhead. Shadowy. The drapes and the hangings eat up all the noise. The banquet room seems miles away instead of just through the archway. Everything's glittery, copper and brass and aluminum. Maybe I've had a bit much to drink.''

"Go on.''

"I kick something. It frightens me. I'm wearing open-toed sandals and I have visions of rodenty creatures. I look down and there's this small leather bag, like a tobacco pouch. I pick it up and realize it isn't tobacco . . .''

"Why?''

"You can't open it. It's sewn shut. And the smell. Sweet. Pungent. Like herbs. A strange smell . . .''

"And then?"

"I look down at the carpet, I imagine to see if there's anything else there. And the skirt of a display table is crooked. All the tables are swathed in that red-and-white-checked French peasant cloth. I think I'll straighten the fabric and I see something . . . something so wrong my heart just stops, seems really to stop."

"What do you see?"

"A shoe. One large black shoe. And it's at an angle, sticking up, so it can't be empty."

"Go on," Spragge said gently. "What do you do?"

"I lift a corner of the cloth, tentatively, with my thumb and my forefinger." Her hands moved but she seemed unaware of it. "I bend down. The light is very bad."

"And?"

"He's there. I find him."

"Joseph Fontenot."

"Yes," Mary said. "With a knife in his chest."

Three

"**S**he confess?"

The paunchy cop gave the question the same emphasis he might have given a request for the time of day. He had kicked the door to the office open, his hands balancing two brown paper sacks and a thermos bottle clutched to his stomach. He didn't seem surprised to find Spraggue seated behind the desk.

"Nah," the cop said, when Spraggue made an effort to stand. "Sit. It's the only decent place to park your ass in this office. I'll set here on the file cabinet. Lieutenant uses the visitor's chair for torture. Shoulda been a special provision against it in the Miranda rules. Your aunt go home?"

"She filled me in a little, then went back to the hotel."

"Too bad. Fine-looking woman. I'm Rawlins, by the way. Detective Sergeant Rawlins."

"Michael Spraggue."

"Well, since your aunt took off, how about if I feed you instead, and then you tell her what a fine cook I am."

"What about Dora's bail?"

22

"Your fancy attorney's attending to it. You didn't answer my question."

"Which one?"

"She confess?"

"I advised her to tell you exactly what she told me," Spraggue said.

Rawlins' eyes narrowed, but his voice stayed unconcerned. "You mean about her secret marriage to Fontenot?"

"Was it a secret to you?" Spraggue asked. "Or did you already know?"

Rawlins snorted, busied himself removing things from the paper bags. "You eat lunch?" he asked.

"No."

When the first bag was empty Rawlins ripped it in half, using the edge of the desk as a paper cutter and spreading the raggedy brown paper across the stained desk blotter. One tablecloth.

"I got about an hour before the lieutenant comes back and I figure to hide out in here and eat my lunch. I always bring plenty and you're welcome to join me."

"My stomach hasn't figured out what time zone it's in yet. I think I'll pass," Spraggue said.

Rawlins removed the cracked red plastic top of the thermos jar and unscrewed the inner seal. He took a big spoon out of the other paper bag, and dished half a white paper goldfish container of rice into the thermos cup. The stuff he poured from the thermos into the red plastic top was basically red, dotted with slivers of green pepper and translucent hunks of onion. It had a smell that grabbed the back of the throat.

"If you want some, just holler," Rawlins said. "It's a gumbo. I make it by the potful and bring it in here. The boys say it melts their teeth, but it's mild to me. It's the cayenne pepper that does that."

"You make it yourself?"

"That's what I said. I'm a lone wolf now. Your aunt live alone?"

There was more than casual interest in the question. Spraggue thought about the bustle of Mary's Chestnut Hill mansion. Pierce, her butler, the fleet of secretaries, housekeepers, the elderly chauffeur.

"Yeah," he said. "She lives alone."

"Widow?"

"In World War Two."

"Long time ago."

"She never remarried."

"You're fond of her?" Rawlins licked the big serving spoon appreciatively before putting it back in the bag.

"She raised me from the time I was fourteen. Fond doesn't even come close."

"Seems a fine woman. Hate to think her cook'd be mixed up in a thing like this. Now your aunt, Mrs. Hillman, would be a pretty rich woman, having her own cook and calling on that Mr. Jackson, who is one hot-ticket attorney, or so I hear."

"Mary Spraggue Hillman. Runs the Spraggue Foundation out of Boston."

"As in Davison Spraggue?"

"Yes," Spraggue said flatly. His robber-baron great-grandfather had a name to conjure with still, years after his death.

"Oh my, yes." Rawlins made a face. "And you're . . . I didn't put it all together. Hell, reckon I'd better quit flirting with her then."

"Please," Spraggue said, "forget about the Foundation. Forget about the old tyrant. It's been a while since anybody's flirted with her. I think she'd love it."

"I don't know. People might take it bad. I don't want folks, least of all you, to get the idea that money buys justice around here."

On Rawlins' round face was the look of suspicion Spraggue had almost gotten used to seeing when people found out he was one of "those" Spraggues. One of the joys of inherited wealth.

Spraggue said, "Is there anyplace I can buy us some coffee? I'll pay for it, if you won't count it as a bribe."

The sergeant's lips spread in a slow grin. "You sure couldn't bribe nobody with the coffee here. It ain't worthy of the name. I bring in my own." He hefted another thermos out of the second sack. "In that first file drawer over there, there's two cups."

The top drawer of a newer file cabinet was sectioned off by a few hanging files. Instead of papers it held packages, small tins, and tiny bottles. Creole mustard. A quart of Tabasco. Stuff so potent the peppery smell was starting to escape. Two hefty mugs were stored under the letter *c*.

"That's my survival drawer," Rawlins explained. "Lieutenant rents it to me in exchange for coffee. If'n I have to eat store-bought stuff at my desk at least I can season it up to where I can taste it."

The coffee was strong, laced with chicory.

"Is this lieutenant in charge of Dora's case?"

"Nope," the sergeant said. "That's me. We work cases on rotation, and my name came up on the roster."

Spraggue said, "So which civic-minded citizen told you about Dora marrying this Fontenot guy?"

"Woman named Denise Michel. Local celebrity."

"She's supposed to be a friend of Miss Levoyer's. Doesn't that strike you as odd behavior for a friend, Sergeant?"

"Nope. Never strikes me that telling the truth to the police is odd behavior."

"Okay. You can make a case for Dora disliking Fontenot, but—" Spraggue started.

"Look, son, I don't make arrests just on motive. Lots of folks hated Joe Fontenot. Everybody I interviewed said he was one son of a bitch. But I got more than motive here, I got the whole rest of the shebang—means, opportunity, the works."

"Could you spell it out?"

"The knife belongs to your Miss Levoyer. She don't deny it. And it's got her prints all over it. That's means as far as I'm concerned."

"Pretty dumb to use such an identifiable weapon."

"I never did see any study of murderers that put 'em in the same class as Rhodes scholars."

Spraggue sipped his coffee.

"And she was right there at that dinner party," Rawlins continued. "Your aunt tell you that? Your Miss Levoyer had opportunity."

"So did a couple thousand other people."

"Not so many as you'd think."

"Hotels are public places."

"Sure are," Rawlins agreed. "But the private rooms at the Imperial Orleans can be pretty damn private. You know they had a guard at the door taking invitations and ticking off the names on a list?"

"But there might have been people who came in through another door."

"No other door to come in through. The two rooms, the ballroom where the dinner was and the second room where the display was, do have separate entrances, so they can be used by two groups, say. But for that night the door from the hallway to the display room was locked. The only entrance was through the main ballroom door, and there was someone on that door all night. The killer was on the invitation list."

"What about the waiters? They didn't come through the main door—and where waiters can pass others can pass."

"True. But the hotel staff isn't a bunch of waiters picked up for a special banquet. There's always a banquet at the Imperial Orleans. And the waiters are well-known."

"That doesn't mean one of them didn't hate Fontenot."

"From what I hear all waiters hate all cooks and vice-versa. We questioned the staff and we were satisfied. And

26

none of them mentioned any extra waiter, anybody unfamiliar.''

"Everybody looks familiar in a waiter's uniform.''

"So you're imagining some impostor waiter, somebody lurking in the kitchen, waiting his chance—''

"It's possible.''

"But it's so fancy,'' Rawlins said. "And right now we got a nice simple solution. I like simple solutions. Nine out of ten times, they're the goods.''

"This is the tenth time.''

"You're so sure about that?''

"How many people were at that dinner?''

Rawlins shrugged. "Eighty.''

"Well, even if nobody extra waltzed in and the kitchen staff is as pure as snow, that's seventy-eight people with as much opportunity as Dora.''

"But only one with that knife. You ask her about that knife.''

"I will, Sergeant.''

"You gonna keep callin' me 'sergeant'?''

"Would you prefer 'detective'?'' Spraggue asked.

"I hate callin' people by what they are instead of who they are. If you call me 'sergeant' or 'detective,' I gotta 'mister' you back. You got a first name, right?''

"Michael.''

"Mine's Gorman, so folks call me 'Rawl' for my last name.''

"Mostly, I'm Spraggue. So folks won't call me 'Mike.' ''

"I'll tell you something, Spraggue. Most murders are pretty damn pat. Wife kills a husband. Husband kills a wife. Most of the time we find the guy standing over the body with the knife or the gun, still wondering what he did. The rest of the time, somebody turns himself in a day or two later, saying I don't know what came over me, but she insulted me something terrible and I couldn't take that, now could I? Most murders are the same damn thing.''

27

Rawlins refilled his coffee mug, dumped in two spoons of sugar, and said, "Look, I'm sorry about this. I'd just as soon have met your aunt on another occasion. But I'm satisfied we got the right person. The D.A. agrees. And that's where my job ends."

"Not necessarily."

"No?"

"You could help me find a loose end to pull at."

"Huh?"

Spraggue slipped a faded photostat out of a plastic sleeve in his wallet, placed it on the desk.

Rawlins fingered the card, read it all the way through. "One Massachusetts private investigator's license, expired," he said. "Your aunt said you were an actor or something."

"Right now, I'm in the 'or something' phase."

Rawlins studied the card. "Six-feet-one. You still weigh one-seventy-five?"

Spraggue shrugged.

"I'm shorter than you, but I sure weigh more. This here says brown eyes and yours look kinda yellow, but I'll pass on that. What it don't say is why anybody with your last name would want a crummy private eye license." The suspicion was back in Rawlins' voice.

"I'd rather be playing Broadway leads. Nobody's offering."

"Is there somebody in Boston who'll vouch for you?"

"Captain Hurley. Homicide."

"I'll check that out."

"I want to see the coroner's report. I'd like to know why you're so damn sure it's Dora's knife. A knife's a knife, and from what Mary said, there were knives all over the room. I'd like to know what Fontenot had on him when he died—"

"You don't want much, do you?"

"I'm just anticipating a little. How long do you think

it's going to take for that high-priced attorney to file a discovery motion?''

"It's, uh, irregular."

"You know, that woman who's stuck in your cell makes the best cup of coffee I've ever tasted."

"She use chicory?"

"Her own blend of beans. Colombian and Kenyan. Grinds it fresh every time."

"Okay," Rawlins said. "Okay. Just do me a favor. Tell your aunt I'm cooperating with you."

"Sure. Now Dora said that Fontenot used a different name when he married her. If a guy uses an alias once, he might do it twice. How about running his prints?"

"Seems a whole lot like blaming the victim to me. Poor guy's dead—"

"That's right. Beyond blame and praise and jail and all that crap. Dora's not."

"Well . . ." Rawlins sucked in a deep breath. "If I do, you'll have to tell your aunt I cook the best gumbo in town. That means you want a taste."

"I'm done with my coffee. Just pour me a little in the same mug."

"Hot" wasn't the word to describe Rawlins' gumbo. It was like a test. Spraggue could feel the heat rise in his throat and his face turn red. When he didn't cough or choke, and he managed a smile, Spraggue knew he'd passed.

Four

"I sure made a mistake on you," Albert Flowers said disgustedly.

The cabbie's name was lettered on the front fender of his battered Oldsmobile. A coffee-colored man with a beguiling grin, he'd already impressed Sprague with his knowledge of the city, his references to the hoodoo power of the charms hanging from his rearview mirror, and his offer of service by the day to the Northerner who had to learn to loosen up and enjoy easy-going New Orleans.

"I think, oh boy, here comes one of them big-spending Yankees," Flowers continued, "just offa the plane and lookin' for a good time. Good man for Albert. Then right off you wanna go to the police station. And now you wanna know about this leather bag that smells funny. Sounds like gris-gris to me."

"Gree-gree? Is that French?" Sprague asked, puzzled. "What's it for?"

Flowers shrugged. "Gris-gris is for a lot of things. You can get a gris-gris to put on a spell, or guard against a spell. You can get one for spirits and one for men. They

30

all different. It depend on who made this one you're talkin' about.''

''And who might have done that?''

''I can't tell you. I couldn't tell by lookin', not even by touchin', and I ain't eager to touch no such thing, no way. But I can tell you this. It cost some money if it's a leather bag. Not somethin' the tourists buy for a lark, somethin' made to order. This gris-gris belong to some guy in the jail? Maybe if you told me what he's been arrested for—''

''He's not in jail,'' Spraggue said. ''He's dead.''

''I guess that gris-gris didn't work so good then,'' Flowers said. ''I doubt, though, the man be lookin' for a refund.''

Spraggue smiled. ''I suppose,'' he said, ''the gris-gris could belong to the man's killer, if he was obliging enough to leave it behind. You said it wasn't the sort of thing a tourist would pick up. It's unusual?''

''Not that strange. Not here among the right sort of people.''

''And if it were found near the body of a man who was a chef here in New Orleans?''

''Nothin' to say a chef can't be interested in a little hoodoo.''

''Is that 'voodoo' or 'hoodoo'?''

''Hoodoo. It's sort of a mix, a mish-mash of voodoo from the islands, all messed up with local Catholic. Your chef, now, he a man of color?''

''White man. Cajun, I think.''

''Be more usual to find a charm like that on a man of color, but we got some white hoodoos here too.''

Spraggue said, ''Maybe you can tell me where I'd be likely to learn something about that charm.''

''Maybe I could.''

''And, of course, if you were assisting me as well as driving, there would be an increase in your pay.''

''Assistin' you in doing what?''

"I'm sort of a private investigator," Spraggue said. The expired-license sort, he added silently.

"You gonna bribe me? Well, okay, I'm easy, I'm easy. I'm just figurin' out the best place to start. I ain't really into no voodoo, no hoodoo, no witchcraft, you know. I keep the charms and stuff, but mostly 'cause the tourists expect it. They want to hear about voodoo, and they want to hear about the graveyards, those spooky-looking tombs, all above ground. Now I hear there's a woman works at this tourist place, this witchcraft museum. Woman named, let me see—Del, yeah, for Delores. Sister Del, she call herself. If we find when she be at work, she can probably send us to somebody who would know about an old leather gris-gris."

"Can you make me an appointment to see this Sister Del?"

"I can sure try."

All the time they were talking, Flowers was driving through streets that narrowed by the block. They crossed a wide boulevard and Spraggue was abruptly oriented, sure of his location. They had found the French Quarter, the *Vieux Carré*, the section of New Orleans he knew from a long ago six-week Tennessee Williams' festival, understudying Brick in *Cat* and Stanley in *Streetcar*, waiting every night for the lead to show up too drunk to go on. Over ten years ago, he figured, startled by how quickly the time had gone. Back then the Quarter had seemed on its way out, its elegant Spanish facades crumbling. Now a renascence was in swing. Fresh paint. New gutters. Old wrought-iron balconies gleamed.

Flowers drove right down Bourbon Street, a feat Spraggue wouldn't have tried drunk or sober. The street never closed; it was one continuous conga line, tourists and natives dancing from one seedy nightclub to the next, one strip joint, one bar, one elegant Creole restaurant, one tourist-trap to another, all stuck together on one street so that the blend of people was even more bizarre than the blend of shops. A dapper man steered a bejeweled woman past a bare-chested tattooed man in motorcycle-leather pants. Hookers leered at cops. Spraggue recalled one Mardi Gras, when he'd been young enough not to mind ten thousand drunks jamming the streets, remembered the faraway glamor, the close-up squalor. He hoped it would come late this year, that this business with Dora would be settled long before Fat Tuesday drove the populace berserk.

"Mardi Gras March the sixth," Flowers offered. "Things startin' to heat up though. Balls every night soon. Good time for a cabbie."

"If you like people throwing up in your cab."

"I don't pick up the ones with the green faces, but sometimes they fool me. I drive plenty careful then. No sharp turns."

The Imperial Orleans had two doormen out front, one to hold the door, the other to stare questioningly at Spraggue's shabby duffel bag and rumpled clothes. The lobby ran to marble floors and pillars, deep-green velvet banquettes, crystal chandeliers. Vases of lilies and freesia made it smell like a place you'd want to stay. The woman behind the desk had a voice so soothing Spraggue almost drowsed off listening to her.

Yes, Mrs. Hillman's suite was number 6L. Yes, she had left a key for the gentleman. Did the gentleman require a bellman? No? The elevator is on your left. Have a pleasant stay.

Mary hadn't said anything at the front desk about a nephew, that was certain from the way the woman looked him over.

He stuck the key into the appropriate door, turned it gently.

Mary yanked the door open, so quickly that she must have been waiting on the far side. She was wearing a rose-colored dressing gown, but her eyes were wide awake.

"I thought you were going to sleep," Spraggue said.

"I did sleep," Mary countered. "A good three hours. I feel absolutely marvelous, ready to dance."

Spraggue closed his eyes and blew out a deep breath. Four hours was a full night's sleep for Aunt Mary. "All I want is food and bed."

"The young have no vitality anymore," Mary replied tartly.

"I'm aging rapidly," Spraggue said. "I may have gone into early retirement when I quit my job to pry into your murder investigation. I smell like a goddamn police station . . . ."

Mary made a faint and maddening noise. "Take a shower and wash the police station off. Your bed and bath are through here. I'll order things from room service. Certainly a hotel that keeps Denise Michel as executive chef should be able to provide an adequate dinner—"

"Denise Michel?"

"What about her?"

"Well," Spraggue said, "she *is* the one who finagled Dora down here. She knew about Dora's marriage to Fontenot. And she kindly told the cops about it. If Dora's innocent, I'd say Denise Michel moves up to number one suspect."

"On the other hand," Mary said, pursing her lips, "let's eat out."

"I doubt she'd poison us in her own hotel."

"Bathe," Mary said sternly. "When your police station aroma has improved, I'll be in my study—through the archway on your right."

The shower helped. He had to admit it. The water—hot, cool, hot, then as cold as he could stand it—pelted him awake. He toweled off briskly in the gold-and-gray splendor of his bedroom, then lifted the phone to check for messages at the desk. None. His agent hadn't caught up with him yet. Maybe he'd finally brought on old Harry's long-overdue cardiac arrest. Walking out of a play the day before opening . . . He wondered what sort of tales his departure would breed. Spraggue? The rich bastard? Oh, yes. Terminally jealous of the lead actor. Couldn't get his lines. An alcoholic, you know. So sad. Not to mention the cocaine . . .

He turned that portion of his mind off, tumbled the contents of his duffel bag on the football-field-sized bed. After yanking on a pair of faded jeans, he draped a towel around his bare shoulders and rubbed a hand across a rough jaw. He tried to remember whether he'd shaved during the morning brouhaha of phone calls, abandonments, airplanes.

Shaved.

He entered Mary's study still rubbing his dripping hair with a towel, half-blinded, but awake. "Hi." He bent and kissed her on the cheek. "Want to start over?"

"You smell marvelous," Mary said. "Did you have a nice flight in?"

"Awful."

"You should have let me send the Learjet."

"No," Spraggue said. "Thanks, but no." He didn't live in the goddamned mansion and he wasn't going to use the goddamned Learjet. His mouth twitched. The commercial flight, late leaving Boston, fogbound in Pittsburgh, had been almost enough to shake his independence. That, and his sinking bank balance. Hollywood hadn't called lately.

Mary smoothly changed the subject. "They have a trout Marguery on the menu that Dora says is quite nice."

"She's out?"

"No, dear. Mr. Jackson, the attorney, is doing all he can, but he wanted to wait for another judge, one who's a trifle less law-and-ordery. Dora mentioned Denise's trout prior to her—uh, incarceration. I ordered two of them and they should be up soon."

"Fine."

"And a bottle of Sauvignon blanc. Possibly I should have made it two bottles."

"Possibly," Spraggue agreed.

"It's bad, isn't it?" Mary said softly.

"I just blew my career, and hired a cabbie to sign me up for hoodoo lessons."

"You know what I mean, Michael. Dora."

"Yeah." Spraggue flopped down on the sofa and closed his eyes.

"So what do you think?" Mary asked. When her nephew didn't answer, she leaned over and placed a thick manila folder on his chest.

Spraggue groaned, but he sat up and thumbed through it with increasing speed. It was stuffed with photographs, newspaper articles, glossy magazine spreads, all tracing the career of Joseph Fontenot.

"Aunt Mary," Spraggue said, "I thought you slept."

"I did," she said. "But first I made a few phone calls. You remember Joanna, the financial writer at the *Globe*? Well, she has a colleague at the *Times-Picayune*. And Pierce came down from Boston."

That explained everything. Pierce, Mary's butler, bridge partner, and chief game opponent, was a wonder, a wizard of organization.

Spraggue pulled a five-by-eight glossy out of the folder. Joe Fontenot had a sleek, rounded face, camouflaged by heavy glasses and a bushy mustache. His weight had smoothed out the age wrinkles and left plump blandness in its place. His ears were tiny, delicate. The collar of his dinner jacket almost touched them, the man had so little in the way of a neck.

"Darling," Mary said, folding her hands in her lap, "I'm your assistant, as well as your client."

Spraggue read the first paragraph of an article headlined CAJUN FOOD GOES HAUTE CUISINE. "Mary," he said, "you ought to go into the business yourself."

"I wish you'd go back to it," she replied. "The Foundation could use a good investigator."

"I'm an actor," Spraggue said. "I avoid reality. Get yourself a license."

36

"How? I do not have three years' investigative experience. Massachusetts requires that, I believe."

"Get your license the way everybody else does. Bribe a politician."

"Another illusion shattered."

"You can't hire me, Aunt Mary. I already have a client."

"Nonsense. I called for help. I expect to pay you for taking on this case."

"So does Dora. People are lining up to throw money at me."

"I'm first in line," Mary insisted.

"Garbage."

"Garbage, yourself. You were acting. And now you're out of a job. And you haven't taken anything from your account with the Foundation in—I don't know how long. What does a good private investigator earn these days?"

"You'd be shocked."

"When was the last time I was shocked?"

"Five hundred a day plus expenses."

"Consider me shocked."

"They don't work all that many days," Spraggue said. "And they give discounts if a case is interesting or involves an old friend."

"I expect to pay regular rates."

"I'll send you a bill," Spraggue said. He wouldn't, but that would stop the argument.

"Good. That's settled then. Where do we start?"

"With the knife," Spraggue said. "Why are they so sure it's Dora's knife?"

"Because it's one-of-a-kind. A French knife that doesn't even have an English name. A *tanqueuer*. A stabbing implement, used for holding a piece of meat against a carving board."

"And why was Dora wandering around with a what's-it?"

"A *tanqueuer*. She brought her entire case of knives

from Boston. Apparently cooks always use their own knives. It would be like me traveling without a toothbrush.''

"But why is Detective Rawlins so sure Dora was the one who used the knife on Fontenot?''

"I can answer that one," Mary said. "I spent quite a while with Rawl—''

"Pet names, already?'' Spraggue raised one eyebrow.

"You see,'' Mary said, ignoring his interruption, "Dora used the *tanqueuer* at her two o'clock seminar. She made steak tartare, and she always chops the meat by hand. Everyone at the seminar saw her use the knife. And saw her replace it in her case. Since she swears she locked the case, and took it up to her room, and put it in her closet, and locked her door—well, you can see that the police would jump to certain conclusions.''

"I'd like a list of the people at the seminar,'' Spraggue said.

"I'll bet,'' Mary said, "that most of them sat at my table at the banquet last night. Remember? I told you they were arguing about knives and food processors and whatnot. Just the sort of argument that could have started at Dora's seminar.''

"Find out. If you're right, the people at your table get to be our prime suspects. With Denise Michel in first place.''

"Do you want me to keep an eye on her?''

"I'd rather you did some financial snooping.''

"Dull, dull, dull,'' Mary said. "Why do I always get stuck with the money angle?''

"Because bank managers make a habit of kowtowing to you.''

"Flatterer. And what will you be up to while I ingratiate myself with silver-haired, silver-tongued bankers?''

"I thought I'd start with the widow. She probably had the best reason for killing Fontenot.''

Mary nodded. "Living with that man cannot have been

pleasant. If I'd spent two evenings with him, instead of one, I might have been tempted to do him in."

"She can tell me more about him. He must have done something to bring on his death, hurt someone, threatened someone . . ."

"I'll try to piece together his life from the articles I've already got," Mary said. "I've been placing them in chronological order. Lots of recent ones. A few early mentions. A gap of about ten years in the middle. I think he was in Europe learning to cook."

"Maybe he married a few more women over there, and they banded together to hunt him down."

"I, for one, think they would have been relieved when he left," Mary said.

"One more thing, Aunt Mary, since you're on such friendly terms with the cops."

"What?"

"Do your best to charm that little leather bag you found at the murder scene away from the good Detective Rawlins. I'd like to see it up close."

Mary ran a hand through her hair. "That shouldn't be too difficult," she said in a self-satisfied tone.

"He's probably just after your money," Spraggue said.

Mary tossed a sofa pillow in his face.

Five

Aunt Mary had pinned the note to the pillow next to his head. She knew how soundly he slept, knew she'd have to drop the bedside lamp from a great height onto bare floor to rouse him.

The note, red felt-tip laced across staid blue stationery, said: *Sleep! What a waste of time! Pierce and I have gone to fetch Dora out of the slammer. Bail is exorbitant. A charming man named Flowers was waiting for you in a cab downstairs so I invited him up. He's having breakfast. Don't forget lunch. One-thirty. Café Creole. Be there.*

The phone shrilled and a Southern twang sang "Wake-up call" in his right ear and promptly hung up. The bedside clock said nine-thirty. He had requested the call for eight. He knew better than to blame the Imperial Orleans operator. No doubt Aunt Mary had decided he needed precisely one and a half hours of sleep more than he himself had planned, and proceeded to rearrange matters to her liking. She could teach the hotel staff a thing or two concerning "imperial."

Spraggue swung his legs over the side of the bed,

grounding his feet in plush carpet. The hum of the air conditioner blurred all other hotel noises. He flicked off the switch and heard machinery, the *tap-tap* of a distant terminal, the *click-click* of a printer—Mary's noises; where she went they followed. Plates clattered. So Albert Flowers was a breakfast guest. He must have impressed Aunt Mary.

Spraggue opened the door and hollered the cabbie's name.

"Yo!" came the response.

"Is there breakfast for me?"

"I been told to order it the minute I hear you."

"Do that," Spraggue said, closing his door.

He lowered himself to the floor, did twenty-five push-ups and fifty sit-ups. He showered, shaved, and dressed in lightweight navy slacks and a light blue button-down Harvard Coop shirt, both wrinkled from their stay in the duffel bag—clothes that left room for improvisation. He wasn't sure who he'd need to be today to get the desired results.

Another note from Mary sat at his place at the breakfast table, folded next to his napkin. The eggs were hot and the note room temperature, so he gave the eggs his attention first. Not just eggs—Eggs Sardou, the breakfast blowout of the old New Orleans planters, poached eggs perched on creamed spinach, slathered with hollandaise. They counteracted his morning exercises and then some.

Albert Flowers had pushed his plate back and was contentedly sipping coffee, white with cream. "Your aunt said to make sure you read this note."

Spraggue lifted one eyebrow. Mary had suborned Flowers, with charm and breakfast.

The note was just an address, but Spraggue knew the workings of his aunt's mind well enough to know that the address would be Jeannine Fontenot's.

"Where's Gretna?" he asked Flowers.

"West Bank. Not far."

He passed the address to Flowers. "You ready?"

"Sure am. Good coffee."

"Let me get a few things and we'll go."

"Okay. I fixed things up with Sister Del. The hoodoo woman, remember? You got an appointment for a reading at nine o'clock tonight."

"A reading?"

"Psychic reading. That's what she calls it."

Spraggue went back to his bedroom and dumped one of the plump down pillows out of its case. He stood for a moment in the center of the room, then moved through the suite, placing an occasional object in the pillowcase.

"You gonna hock that stuff?" Flowers followed him around anxiously. "Your aunt say it's all right?"

"These are theatrical props," Spraggue said, prompted by Flowers' quizzical glance. "Never mind. Let's go."

Within the Quarter, traffic stood still. The acrid tar smell, the haze, the jitter and boom of construction machinery told the tale. Every alternate street was being ripped up and repaved. Jagged hunks of cement lurched out of vast potholes. Flowers cursed, and finally drove up on the sidewalk to escape Royal Street. Spraggue, in the front seat, cranked the window down and watched barges slide along the wide brown Mississippi as the cab crossed the bridge.

The address was in the middle of a block bleached by too much sun, a block that housed both a corner liquor store and a church. Number 18, a ramshackle structure of indeterminate architecture, was too big to be a private home. If the neighborhood decayed any further, it would end as a funeral parlor.

The surrounding blight had been temporarily defeated. The light blue paint was so new it shone. A lacy wrought-iron balcony wound around the second story, giving the place a French Quarter air. The sign out front was neon— enormous script letters spelled out *Fontenot's*.

The name of the place didn't surprise Spraggue. Sergeant Rawlins had given Mary a list of the contents of the dead man's pockets. Mixed in with the keys and credit cards were two items of interest: five one-hundred dollar bills, and a fully written acceptance speech for the Great Chefs of New Orleans Best Chef Award. The speech was not modest. If Fontenot had gotten a chance to deliver it, the audience might have taken turns stabbing him.

Mrs. Fontenot answered the doorbell on the first ring, blinking in the sunshine.

She wore a crisp pleated white cotton blouse tucked into a dark full skirt, making the most of a waist too small for one so buxom. Her features were strong, her face carefully made up, a mask that almost hid reddened eyes. Over forty, he thought, good skin, good bones. Her dark hair was scraped back from her broad forehead and twisted up on top of her head. She had an air of brisk forcefulness about her that made Spraggue wonder if she had slept since the murder; she looked like the kind of person who handled disaster by taking every item out of a closet, dusting it, and putting it back.

"Oh, God," she said. "I've been expecting you." There was a weary eagerness to her voice. "Which paper did you say you were from?"

There. That was why good acting coaches always said not to prepare for an improv.

"Times," he muttered quickly. Surely the most likely candidate would be the Louisiana *Times-Picayune.* If he were wrong, his error could be fobbed off as a request for the correct time—or an excuse for his presumed tardiness.

"I never thought—" she began enthusiastically, then calmed her voice to a more funereal pace. "Me, I always read these stories in the paper while I'm waiting on line by the market. You know: 'Mother of Murdered Girl Speaks Out,' but I never thought I'd be talking to a reporter about my own husband, struck down in the prime of life."

Wrong paper, Spraggue thought. Mrs. Fontenot sounded like she'd memorized one of the turgid soap opera scripts his agent kept sending him. Her words had a strange sort of rhythm, an unfamiliar melody that reminded him of other voices, Dora's lilting French, Rawlins' twangy Southern.

43

"What paper did you way you were from?" she repeated.

"The *Star*," he hastily amended.

"I mostly read the *Enquirer*," she said apologetically. "This was going to be our restaurant." She motioned him inward. "You said you might take some photographs . . . The kitchen was my husband's own design. If you had a camera . . ."

"I was just going to ask where I could find the nearest drugstore," Spraggue said smoothly. "My photographer's out of film. If I can send him for supplies, we can take care of the whole story this morning."

"Wonderful. I was worried you might not make it until late this afternoon, like you said. Hmmmm. A drugstore. How about a regular camera store? There's one close by." She pointed off toward a distant intersection and said, "It's just three blocks east of the light. Right by the KB. Big place. Can't miss it."

"Thanks." Spraggue hoped the "other" reporter would get called to a fire. He went back out to the cab, gave detailed instructions to the rear window, trusting the glare to hide the fact that only Flowers was inside.

He opened the cab's front door, rummaged in the pillowcase, and came out with a notebook, two pens for his breast pocket, and the cassette recorder he always traveled with when he was acting. He'd stuffed it in his luggage by mistake, from force of habit, ready to record his lines and cues. Now he was glad of the error. Grasping the recorder, he realized he felt comfortable in the reporter role. He'd played one in a TV cop show once. Then he'd worn horn-rimmed glasses and a cap.

"Come right in," Mrs. Fontenot said when he climbed back onto the porch.

The foyer was dark and cool, and smelled of newly varnished wood floors. Several interior walls had been knocked down to make one large main dining area. Ceiling fans spun lazily overhead. The decor was haphazard, here and there a stab at elegance: flocked red wallpaper, gold wall sconces. But the floors were bare, and the walls covered with unframed maps and menus. Chairs and tables were crowded into the room as if Fontenot had anticipated an overflow crowd. The overall effect was contradiction, a ritzy diner.

"I can just hear my Joe say how fine the publicity would be." Mrs. Fontenot let out a mournful sigh. "Only now, I don't know. I doubt I'll ever open this place. People would have come out to Gretna to eat Joe's cooking. Yes, they would. They would've come miles and miles. Me, I'm a good cook myself. Pretty near good as Joe. But I haven't got Joe's reputation and now, well, I don't know if I've got the strength."

Spraggue made sympathetic noises and scribbled in his notebook.

"I suppose I could sell it," she went on. "But it would seem like, oh, such a betrayal. Joe worked so damned hard for this place. It was his great dream. Just come see the kitchen."

Spraggue got a guided tour, complete with relics (Fontenot's favorite cast-iron griddle) and anecdotes (the time Fontenot had made bread pudding with bourbon and lemon sauce for, well, a very well-known actress who's a trifle overweight, and she—well, Mrs. Fontenot wouldn't want that in the paper!). Joe Fontenot hadn't skimped in his kitchen; his restaurant was either deep in debt or well-endowed. His wife waxed eloquent over the eight-burner Vulcan gas ranges and the stacks of skillets. For a time she seemed to forget entirely the reason for his visit. Her plain face beamed and all the sharp separate parts blended into a whole that could only have been called attractive. She conjured up opening night, the first delighted customers—and then she remembered, and her face fell into sober defeated folds.

"And you and your husband lived here as well?" Spraggue prompted.

"On the second floor. We haven't done a thing up there. All our time, all our energy, went into the restaurant."

"I'd like to see your own place. Kind of a homey angle for the story."

"But it's a mess. Boxes still packed, no pictures on the walls—"

"I understand, Mrs. Fontenot. I won't take any photos."

She shrugged, as if no one could possibly understand. But she gave in, saying, "Well, at least up there, I can make some coffee. You'd like some coffee?"

"Very much."

"I don't think you told me your name. Or if you did, I don't remember."

"Ed," Spraggue said. "Ed Adams." It came to him as he said it that the name was from some forties Alan Ladd film noir, a journalist who found a body in a cheap hotel room.

"You're not from around here."

"No."

"I can tell by the accent."

Spraggue wasn't used to thinking of himself as having an accent.

Upstairs, the paint was dingy yellow. No pictures on the walls, as Mrs. Fontenot had pointed out, but you could tell where the last tenants had hung theirs by the faded rectangles. The windows had plain white shades, no curtains. All the furniture looked hand-me-down—springs sprung, upholstery tattered.

"We were going to do so much up here," Jeannine Fontenot shouted from the tiny galley kitchen. "I found the most perfect wallpaper, pale blue with yellow roses. We were going to furnish from scratch, just throw all this junk out."

More money, Spraggue thought. He studied two Plexiglas-framed photographs on the dusty coffee table. One was Joseph Fontenot; the other a faded snapshot of a small child, a girl, as the frilly white dress and elaborate ringlets made clear. She smiled up at the photographer with such joyful innocence that Spraggue hated to think of her growing up.

"Now," Fontenot's widow said, settling onto the couch with a mug of chicory-flavored coffee in one hand, "what do you want me to tell you?"

"Everything," Spraggue said easily. "Background. I hope you don't mind the tape recorder. It helps my memory and I want to get any quotes just right. Anything that you say is off the record will stay off the record." He smiled down at her and wondered if he weren't overdoing the smarminess just a bit. His image of one of those gossip-sheet "reporters" was pretty negative, sort of a greased eel. If he'd had time to costume the part he would have chosen a shiny suit and a loud tie.

"I guess it'll be okay. Makes me a little bit nervous. What do you mean by background?"

"I want to do the sort of piece that will let our readers know exactly what kind of a man your husband was. Where he came from. How he lived. His accomplishments. When someone is killed in such a spectacular fashion, right before the presentation of an award he might have won—"

"*Would* have won. No 'might' about it. In the category of best chef, my husband might as well have been running alone. There was no one close."

Mrs. Fontenot did have something in common with her husband—a belief that he could do no culinary wrong. She bit her lip and continued, "Maybe that's why . . ."

"Why what?"

She thought about her words before she spoke, and then she pitched her voice low, as if a whisper would outwit the tape recorder. "There is so much jealousy in this place. You wouldn't think it. You would think there would always be room for one more, for a man or woman of talent and taste and style. But my husband—you wouldn't think it to meet him, he was such a charming man . . ."

That would take some convincing, judging by that acceptance speech, and by Mary's assessment of the man.

"He was charming," Jeannine Fontenot repeated in her tense whisper, "but a lot of the other chefs didn't appreciate him, because—well, it's the truth and not boasting, he was better than they were."

"And you think that—?"

"I know what you're going to ask. Do I think that one of those other cooks killed him out of jealousy, out of spite?"

"Do you?"

"This part I want off the record," she said. "But yes. Yes, me, I think there may be something in that. Jealousy is a very powerful feeling."

She said the last few words with such intensity that Spraggue wondered how much she'd known about her husband and Dora.

"Now," she said apologetically. "I've gotten way off the track. You wanted to start with my husband's background?"

"Please, I'm interested in your theories about his death."

She wasn't to be led. She mumbled that possibly they could go back to that later.

Spraggue said, "Maybe I could start with the education of a great chef. Was your husband raised in a family that cared about cooking?"

She laughed. "He was raised in a family that cared about eating. Talk about poor! They didn't have a pot to cook jambalaya in. My husband was born in the bayou. Bayou Cajun, like me."

That identified the elusive accent. Spraggue was glad he was getting it on tape.

"He was the youngest," she went on, "the only boy, and a wild one at that. Funny, with all those women, he was the one wound up doing the cooking. He always said if I'd ever tasted his mother's cooking, I'd know why he cooked—out of self-defense. He always had a nose for food. You know, great cooks don't smell or taste the way other people do. It's a gift, the way that perfect pitch is a gift. It's an art. People in New Orleans appreciate that more than the rest of this country, almost the way they do in France.''

"Your husband's parents, are they still alive?''

"No. No. That Cajun bayou life moves fast. The girls are married and mothers at seventeen. At fifty they're old, the way that others are at eighty. His parents died years ago. And his sisters are all married off, out of touch. Not a close family, like some. He had a half-brother—or was he a step-brother? Just about Joe's age. They were real close, T-Bob and Joe, growing up. Two of the three musketeers. We owe a lot to T-Bob.''

"T-Bob? Why T?''

"You don't know Cajun. A mixture of French, English, some words all our own. T-Bob was probably named for his father, and they would call him 'Petit Bob,' you know, Little Bob. And that would become 'T-Bob.' ''

"I see.''

"But what T-Bob's last name would be, I don't even remember.''

She was starting to talk to herself.

"You said you owed this T-Bob a lot,'' he said.

She looked up at him in surprise, as if she had forgotten he was there.

"We owe him the restaurant,'' she said simply, "the dream. All this is our legacy from T-Bob. He was so close to my husband.''

"Your husband must have been very sad to lose such a friend.''

"Well, it had been a long time since he'd seen T-Bob.'' She hesitated uncomfortably. "And the money, it was a wonderful surprise, the answer to so many prayers.''

"When was this? When did T-Bob die?''

"I'm not sure when he died, but the money came maybe

six months ago. We did a lot in six months, finding this place, changing it—"

"You mentioned 'three musketeers.' Your husband and T-Bob and . . . ?"

"It's a long time ago," she said. "I have a bad memory for names. You wanted to know about my husband's cooking?"

Spraggue smiled blankly, inwardly cursing Mrs. Fontenot's devotion to the straight line. "When did your husband start to cook for a living?"

"Friends would always happen to drop in at meal time if they knew Joseph was cooking. They'd bring something for the pot. You know, 'I got a rabbit. If your boy Joseph wants to season up a rabbit stew like he knows how to make so special, my family'd sure be happy to help y'all eat it.' He learned to cook with nothing and he had no training. He made things up as he went along. Whatever got trapped, he cooked. Later, of course, he had formal training, in France."

"Before you were married?"

"No. No. Nothing happened before we were married. He was only eighteen when we married, and me, I was one week past my seventeenth birthday." The shadow of a smile flickered across her face, and for the first time, Spraggue had a sense that she must have loved the murdered man.

But how long ago?

"I see," he said. It was a verbal nod, a prompt—and she went on.

"We live the way our parents live. We speak mostly Cajun French and we trap and catch fish and get by. There's always enough to eat, but it's a long way from where we started to here, believe me."

"This is terrific coffee," Spraggue said encouragingly. He wondered how much blank tape was left on the cassette.

"Thank you," she said. "It is quite a story but it's not

50

my story. It's Joe's story. There was always more that he wanted. He wasn't happy in the bayou, always dreaming big city, and not Abbeville either. Dreaming Paris. And one day he says to me he must go to France. "He says, 'Would you be okay on your own for a while?' See, we didn't have money for us both to go. You know, he says, 'I'll come back for you,' but I gotta learn something else. I can't spend my life here."

She paused, lost in an earlier time.

"It was hard for me when he left. I thought I'd die, and the baby, well . . ." She smiled at the photograph on the coffee table. "The baby was so young. Me, I have my family and I knew he'd come back—but I didn't think he would be so long away."

"How long?" Spraggue said quickly, thinking of the missing years Aunt Mary hadn't been able to chart.

"Oh," Jeannine said, uncomfortable again, "a long time."

"And during that time what did your husband do?"

"All the things he dreamed about, I guess. He lived in Paris and he learned to be a chef. He lived all over France."

And in New Orleans with Dora. "He wrote you?"

She swallowed coffee. "My husband is not—was not a writing man."

"But you waited."

"He said he'd come back and he did. I almost didn't know him at first—he'd been sick. But after a while, when he was strong again, we packed up and came to New Orleans and he got a job as a cook, and he worked very hard and became so well known—and then his own restaurant, and there was gonna be a cookbook with a fancy New York publisher—and now—"

The doorbell rang. It echoed through the downstairs restaurant like a Chinese gong.

"That must be my photographer," Spraggue said. Or the real reporter, he thought.

"Oh." Mrs. Fontenot pushed at a few stray hairs on her forehead, tested out a smile. "Would you want pictures just of the restaurant or—"

"It would be wonderful if we could include you in a few shots. If you wouldn't mind."

"Well . . ." she said uncertainly.

"Think about it," Spraggue urged as they went down the stairs. "I wouldn't want you to do anything that would make you uncomfortable." He shuddered slightly as he said it. Was there nothing this reporter fellow wouldn't stoop to?

The door opened on a Flowers transformed, a Flowers whose experience of professional photographers must have been bizarre indeed.

He wore what could have been a flak jacket from an old Army movie, and had so much paraphernalia strung and strapped about his person that he had to slide sideways through the door. A light meter swung from his neck like an oversized medallion. Thirty-five-millimeter film cans hung on his belt like shells on a bandolier. He sported mirrored sunglasses, and he was all brisk cheerfulness.

"What kind of shots you have in mind?" he asked Spraggue immediately, nodding a hello at Jeannine Fontenot. "*House Beautiful* spread?" He was terse and businesslike, a pro. He was having a great time.

"Get a few shots of each room," Spraggue said. "I'll trust your judgment." Under his breath, he added, "Take your time."

As long as Flowers was going to play along with such gusto, he'd see what personal items he could find up in the apartment. He patted his back pocket absent-mindedly and said, "I'll be down in a minute. I dropped my notebook upstairs."

This last was untrue, but Mrs. Fontenot was already engaged with Flowers, discussing camera angles. Spraggue wondered if Flowers could take pictures. He certainly talked a good game.

Once upstairs, Spraggue wondered how long he could justify searching for a lost notebook. He tucked it under a sofa cushion.

The brown cardboard boxes stacked in one corner were labeled, but the masking tape stickers told only the room each should be deposited in: SECOND FLOOR LIVING ROOM was all the information they gave. The tape fastening the top box was loose, so Spraggue helped it along.

Books. Large ones. At first he thought they were all cookbooks, but one, stuck in vertically, had the thickness of a scrapbook.

A photograph album. An old one judging by the yellowed leaves. Yes. If that were Mrs. Fontenot, it would have to be, oh, twenty years old. He thumbed through the pages quickly. Joe Fontenot liked taking pictures of his wife. He took a decent snapshot. Had she been his wife yet? She had a photogenic smile. Sheet after sheet of Jeannine Fontenot. Then sheet after sheet of the daughter, the little girl in the coffee table photograph, the pictures markedly fuzzier.

The telephone rang. Spraggue stuck the book back in the cardboard box and resealed the tape. Two rings and it died, answered below in the restaurant. He breathed again.

Then he started down the hall.

A kitchen, a bedroom, a bath. Would all Fontenot's papers still be packed in brown cartons?

Flowers raised his voice so that Spraggue could hear him from the stairwell. "Well, I'd like to get some more shots of the kitchen, but if you're sure that's all . . ."

Spraggue turned and fled back to the living room. He flipped the safety catch on a back window open. The shade, after he pulled it down another half inch, hid the lock. Then he knelt in front of the sofa and thrust his hand under the cushion.

"There," he said triumphantly, pulling out the notebook and turning when he heard footsteps on the stairs. "It must have slid down here. You didn't have to worry about me."

Mrs. Fontenot was jumpy. Either the phone call or Flowers had upset her. "No," she said hurriedly, "it's not that. It's just that I didn't realize the time. I have to ask you to leave now."

He held out the tape recorder. "But I still have a few questions."

She stared at her wristwatch. "A couple more," she said.

"You know they've arrested a woman, Dora Levoyer, for your husband's murder."

"I was told that."

"Did the police tell you why they arrested her?"

"Turn that machine off."

"Okay."

"Yes, I know what they say, that this woman was his mistress long ago—"

"His wife."

"Ridiculous. I don't believe it. That's all. I think it's easier to arrest her than to look for the jealous one, the one who couldn't stand my husband's success. This woman, this Miss Levoyer, she's not from around here, she's not well known. The police want to keep this nice and quiet. I don't believe it. That's all."

"Who else would you suggest I talk to, to get a complete picture of your husband?"

"Well, you could talk to Paul Armand. At the Café Creole. He worked with Joe. He can tell you about Joe's cooking."

"And?"

"Oh, a lot of cooks around here. Talk to the people at the Great Chefs, they'll tell you he would have won."

"What about Denise Michel?"

"No. She hardly knew him. She didn't like him. You wouldn't get anything from her."

"Didn't like your husband? Do you know why?"

"That's enough questions."

"Did your husband own a gris-gris, a sort of charm he kept with him?"

"Did the police tell you that? Look, he had a charm, but it meant nothing—like a rabbit's foot. My husband was a good Catholic."

Spraggue shrugged, said, "I'd like to talk to your daughter, for the article."

"No."

"It would give our readers another angle."

"No. My daughter should not be bothered with this. It would upset her."

"Is she away at school? She's seventeen, isn't she?"

"Eighteen. She's not away anywhere. But I don't want you to interview her. She's been through enough. There will be nothing in this article about my daughter, you understand, or there will be no article at all."

"But—"

"Look, I have been polite to you at a time of grief. I answered your questions because I think that people should know that jealousy killed my husband. I've let you take pictures." Mrs. Fontenot sneaked another look at her thin gold wristwatch. "And now I ask you to leave."

Six

Flowers held it in until they slammed the doors of the cab shut—barely. Then he gave a great whoop and asked eagerly, "How'd I do, man? How'd I do?"

"Nice work. I wish you could have held her down there longer. I wanted to find Fontenot's checkbook. He was carrying five hundred bucks when he died, and it would give me a warm feeling to know it didn't come legit from his checking account."

"I tried," Flowers said. "Once she got that phone call, she was different. Before that call, she was fussin' with her hair and all ready to let me snap pictures to my heart's content. After that call, all she wanted was to send me on my way."

"Well, you did fine. Authentic. Where'd you get the camera gear?"

Flowers slapped the pillowcase on the front seat. "Theatrical props, right? Got 'em from my brother-in-law. He lives kinda close by and I busted records gettin' over there. Gotta get the goods back tonight, though, or my sister's in big trouble."

"You actually take any pictures?"

Flowers bristled. "Course I did! And my brother-in-law'll develop 'em—for a price. I took the layout, you know, like a bank job, like if we was gonna break in later. Shot the doors and windows. Took a close-up of the front door lock—"

"You have true criminal instincts."

"I had me one hell of a time," Flowers said. "You need an assistant full time, you let me know."

"Up in Boston?"

"Not durin' the winter time."

"That may limit the partnership."

Flowers' enthusiasm was undiminished. "Well, what are we gonna do now?"

"Why did she clear us out so fast?" Spraggue said under his breath.

"I tol' you, 'cause of that phone call."

"Who was it from?"

"Dunno."

"You listen in?"

"Sure," Flowers said.

"She must have called the other person something. Think. When she answered the phone, she said hello, and then . . ."

"Honey!" Flowers said triumphantly. "She called him 'honey'!"

"Ah," Spraggue said. "Maybe we'd better wait here for a while."

"It's a lover, right?" Flowers asked. "You think it's her lover, this 'honey'? You think maybe she offed her old man 'cause she had somethin' else goin' on the side?"

"I think it's the daughter. She didn't want me to talk to her daughter. And if dear daughter called to say she was on her way over and Momma didn't want our paths to cross—"

"You think the daughter killed her daddy?"

"Momma doesn't want us to talk to her. Any time any-

57

body doesn't want me to talk to somebody, that somebody zips to the top of my interview list."

Flowers grinned.

Spraggue stared at his watch. "Trouble is, I've got a lunch date."

A dark green Volkswagen Rabbit eased into the alley beside the restaurant.

The driver moved quickly, with a young woman's step. She ran up the front stoop and knocked, then disappeared inside. Spraggue scribbled the license number of the green Rabbit in his phony reporter's notebook, then turned to Flowers. "If I leave you here to keep tabs on Fontenot's daughter, can you call another cab to get me back to the Quarter?"

"I could. Waste of time though. Just mosey yourself 'round the block to Le Ruth's. 'Round lunchtime, every tourist in the Quarter cabs out there. Any of them drivers be delighted to have a return fare."

"Okay."

"And I'll eyeball this lady for you. What you want to know about her?"

"Where she lives. Where she works. Where I can find her if I want her."

The cabbie chortled. "Follow that dame, right?"

"You got it," Spraggue said. "Then catch me at the hotel in time for that hoodoo ceremony tonight."

Seven

"Paul Armand will join us for dessert," Aunt Mary said contentedly, dabbing at one corner of her mouth with a linen napkin.

"Dessert?" Spraggue spread a hand protectively over his stomach. "Look, if you made any dinner plans for me, cancel them. I may want to act again, and Falstaff is the only good fat-man part I know."

"I've never seen you grill a suspect," Mary said brightly. "I'm looking forward to it."

The Café Creole was hardly the setting for the third degree. The restaurant made Fontenot's place look like a corner cafeteria. Satiny rose-colored wallpaper spread upward from dark-panelled wainscoting. Chandeliers glowed overhead. The main dining room was a fantasy ballroom heisted from a wealthy planter's antebellum manse, complete with an overflow of ladies and gentlemen waiting for tables. The line wandered clear out to Bourbon Street and down the block, where the elegantly garbed queue could gawk into two strip joints, one featuring an "all-male kick line," the other a "live college girl revue," and an open-air saloon where a Cajun fiddler stomped and wailed on a make-shift stage.

Spraggue hadn't liked leapfrogging the line, but Mary had assured him that all the regular patrons did it, and they'd been ushered immediately and ceremoniously to a table where a bottle of champagne waited, compliments of Monsieur Armand. The starch-stiff waiter with the waxed mustache had not failed to notice this courtesy and the service had been, like the oysters Bienville and the soft-shell crabs, exemplary. Dining out with Mary was like that. Something in her demeanor called forth the best efforts of waiters and cooks alike. Maybe she looked like a restaurant reviewer.

"Can I help?" she asked eagerly. "With Armand?"

"Just be interested," Spraggue said.

"I am."

"If he's a talker, let him talk. Talkers are always looking for listeners. If he's not the chatty type, we crank the interest level a little higher. I've seen you do it when you deal with your money men. Suddenly you hang on their every word—"

"That's just common sense—" Mary began.

"That's acting," Spraggue said.

When Paul Armand crossed the room, heads followed. There was a faint murmur as savvy diners recognized the chef and whispered his identity to their table mates. He was a tall man with a stooped posture that made him look as if he'd been caught bending over to stir a sauce pot. He must have been lean once, but age and haute cuisine were catching up with him in the form of a protruding belly, which he sometimes remembered to hold in. Now, aware that eyes were on him, wrapped as he was in chef's apron, his graying hair topped with a tall white toque, he made the effort, straightened himself, and was altogether an imposing figure with his thin, drawn face and bushy eyebrows.

He sketched a courtly little bow in Mary's direction.

60

From his name and appearance, Spraggue expected a French accent, possibly fake, but Armand's voice was pure deep South, broad and lilting. "Miz Hillman? Pleased to meet you again, and I do hope the circumstances are more congenial this time than last—though I doubt the food could be as fine."

Mary returned his formality. "Mr. Armand, I'd like you to meet my nephew, Michael Spraggue. The cooking at the awards banquet was exquisite, but I have found nothing to complain of here."

His gallantries accepted, Armand sank into a chair and the paunch came out of hiding. He said, "You're a cook yourself?"

"No," Mary replied, "but I am an avid eater, and I don't know where or if I've tasted a finer sauce than the one on this soft-shell crab."

"Ah." Armand smiled. His fingers were busy on the table, automatically aligning the silverware in front of him precisely one inch from the table's edge. "You're one dangerous lady. You've got me totally disarmed, and I'll tell you whatever it is you want to know. Now you said you were working for that woman who's accused of killing poor Joseph. Denise told me the whole story, how she used to be married to Joe and all, or thought she was, anyhow. I think the cops are way off base, but I don't see how I can help."

Poor Joseph. Spraggue regarded the man with interest. Had he found a friend of Joe Fontenot's, someone who mourned his passing?

"I already ordered dessert," Armand said abruptly as waiters began hovering. "First, something from the cheese tray, a *chèvre* with just a bit of cinder, then an assortment of tiny French fruit tarts, and *café filtre.*"

Mary nodded happily and Spraggue thought of another fat male role—Big Daddy in *Cat on a Hot Tin Roof.* He said to Armand, "You sound as if you were a friend of Fontenot's."

"I surely was," Armand answered gravely. His eyes never left the hands of the waiters. One young waiter, aware of the intense scrutiny, almost dumped the "*chèvre* with the hint of cinder" on the rug.

"What can you tell me about him?" Spraggue said.

"To help get that lady out of jail?"

"Dora Levoyer," Mary reminded him. "She was at our table at the awards dinner."

"The name slipped my mind. She is—or she was—one fine cook. Lost track of her. Haven't heard that name for some time."

"She no longer cooks for the restaurant trade," Mary said. "She's in private service. My own."

"Ah." Armand's bushy eyebrows lifted and settled. "Then she works for you and not the other way around—and I take your compliment about my soft-shell crab even more highly. Now bear with me a minute. I thought the police had the whole thing tied up with a ribbon."

Spraggue said, "We don't think Dora killed anyone."

"I think you're right." Armand sighed and flicked a stray crumb of French bread off the tablecloth with a well-manicured fingernail. "But if she didn't, well, that surely could open a couple cans of worms around here."

"Maybe we could start with how you came to know Joseph Fontenot," Spraggue said.

"I miss him," Armand said quietly, as if he were embarrassed to acknowledge the fact. "And I'm surprised that I do. Joe was a difficult man, such a difficult man—but he was an artist in his own way, and yeah, I guess I miss him. Maybe it's the shock. Guess it's like losing a bit of my own life, I knew him so long. Some of it's mourning for myself. Somebody close to you dies like that, it makes you realize that someday everybody will say these nice things about you—and these nasty things, too—and you won't be able to get back at 'em. Makes me feel old."

A talker, all right, Spraggue thought.

"How long did you actually know him?" he asked.

Maybe this was someone who could fill in the missing years.

"Since I was a kid. I knew him from the bayou. I knew his people. He was the one who was going to be the famous chef—but I made it first, and he came to me for a job."

"When was that?"

Armand wrinkled his brow and pouted his lips, deep enough in thought to get careless about his looks. "Eight, nine years ago. Maybe a bit longer—I can never remember exactly when things happen. But I hadn't seen him in a long time."

"How long?"

"Long enough so I didn't even recognize him. God, people change. The glasses and the gimpy leg. He looked like he'd had hard times, and my restaurant was doing well. Once, I think, when I was still a boy, teenager maybe, I told him if he ever needed work to come to me. See, I wasn't born in the bayou like him. I used to go down with an uncle of mine to trap and fish. My rich uncle, Joe always called him, because a man who owns a boat must be very rich. Joe would show us the spots to catch the best crawfish, the best *sac-a-lait*—that's perch—things like that. We used to yap a lot about growing up, the way boys do, and in my dream my rich uncle would die and I'd open a fine restaurant and Joe would cook for me. In his dream, he'd find a pot of gold, or marry a rich girl, and open his own. My dream came true faster."

Armand sampled a forkful of raspberry tart and nodded curt approval. A waiter ceased hovering and disappeared.

"At first," Armand continued, "I could hardly believe this man was the same person as that boy, but when I tasted his gumbo, I knew he was the same old Joe."

"Did Fontenot get along well with the rest of the staff here?"

Armand lifted his eyes from his careful dissection of the raspberry tart. "If I said so, the others would sure give me the lie," he admitted. "Joe was difficult, that's all there was to it."

"How?"

"Well . . ." The eyebrows did their lift-and-settle routine. "He was special. He was gifted. And I guess he thought there oughta be a different standard of conduct for the creative chef. He put himself above the others. Now, I wanna say that he *was* gifted. In a man with no gift, his actions would have been intolerable. But, well, Joe knew what he could get away with. He knew that we could afford to lose some old salad chef, some apprentice saucier, a whole lot easier than we could afford to lose him. Because he was good. He was special. I guess we all wished he didn't have to remind everybody how special he was all the time."

"He had arguments with the rest of the staff?" Sprague asked.

Armand threw back his head and laughed. Sprague found himself thinking that the laughter was as rigidly controlled as the rest of the man's behavior.

"Arguments!" Armand repeated. "Since Joe left, my kitchen's been like a library. Nobody hollers anymore. It used to be like a Cajun bar during Mardi Gras. Of course, part of the lull may be because I'm in there now, and the cooks are a little scared of me. Since Joe left, I do more of the cooking."

"How long ago did he leave?"

"About six months. I always knew that when he had enough money, he'd open his own place. God knows, he saved as much as he could from his salary here, scrounged as many meals offa me as he could."

"You don't sound as if you minded."

"Couldn't blame him. I always wanted my own place, too. And there's plenty of room in New Orleans for another fine restaurant. Other cities, maybe not. But here, everybody eats out, and the competition only helps. If people eat at Fontenot's, then they come back here to see if I'm

64

still as good, and they can't quite tell, so they have to go back to Fontenot's to check, and then they have to come back here—you see?''

''Jeannine Fontenot doesn't think many of the restaurant owners of New Orleans agree with you on that.''

''Oh, Jeannine. She tooting that jealousy horn again? How everybody's against her Joe? Well, she'll see. When she opens that place up, she'll have a crowd every night and it won't hurt us a bit.''

''She didn't seem to think she'd be opening at all, without Joe to draw people in.''

''Bullshit!'' Armand mouthed the second syllable of the word, with a quick look over at Mary to see if he'd offended her. ''Maybe you don't know how fine a cook that lady is. You know she wasn't at that banquet 'cause she's Joe's little woman. Maybe Joe got her thinking that, but she was there in her own right, as one of the Great Chefs of New Orleans. Hell, otherwise I'd have brought my wife, if she could've got the time off work.''

''Does your wife cook?'' Mary slipped the question in.

''She's a nurse. Always pulling down night shifts.''

Spragrue asked, ''Do you know how Fontenot got the money to open his restaurant?''

''Savings, far as I know. He worked hard. I paid him well and he was tight with a buck. You want another one of these tarts before your coffee?''

''No, thanks,'' Spragrue said. ''They're wonderful, but I couldn't eat another—''

''I'd love one,'' Mary said.

''Apricot or raspberry?''

''Apricot.''

''Coffee?''

''Please.''

''Did you ever hear Fontenot talk about a relative of his, a half-brother or step-brother named T-Bob?'' Spragrue barely got the question in before they were surrounded by waiters. Mary's plate was refilled. His own plate disappeared and a coffee cup capped with a tiny silver filter pot took its place.

"T-Bob?" Spraggue repeated.

"Sounds familiar," Armand said. "I don't recall."

Spraggue said, "Did Fontenot come into any sort of legacy before he left here?"

"If he did, he didn't tell me about it. But come to think of it, that would explain the size of that new restaurant. I thought he'd start small, not with a monster like that place. I figured he'd taken out a loan—and a sizable one at that. I thought maybe he had a friend who was a banker. Or else . . ."

"Or else?"

"This is just something I picked up in the kitchen. Cooks gossip, you know. Chop a little, gab a little, stir a little, talk a little. Anyhow, I did hear that Joe went and presented a cookbook idea to Simon and Schuster. You know, the publisher that does Denise Michel's cookbooks. And there was talk that Fontenot was about to replace Michel as the local cookbook millionaire. I thought maybe . . ."

"Maybe?" Spraggue prompted.

"Well . . ." Armand seemed reluctant to continue, but then the words started pouring out in a rush. "I just wondered, I thought maybe some deal of his had fallen through, either the cookbooks or a bank loan or something."

"What made you think he'd had a disappointment?" Mary asked. "I thought he seemed fairly pleased with himself at the banquet."

"Oh, he did. No doubt about that," Armand said. "But that could've been pride. Joe was one proud man. A flamboyant man. Never missed a chance to talk about how he came from nobody and nothin' to be the best chef in New Orleans. It was after he died, you know. I kept thinkin' about who could've done it. And comin' up empty. And I wondered if the police weren't missin' the point. It's a terrible thing to say, terrible as murder, but I keep wonderin' if Joe did it himself. I mean, he worked so hard for

66

that restaurant and if he knew something was gonna keep him from opening it . . . Money trouble, maybe. Or if he had some awful disease. Cancer . . .''

"Suicide by knife isn't all that common," Mary said.

"I know. But Joe was familiar with knives, used to knives."

"Was he the kind of man who'd stage his own death to get somebody else in hot water?" Spraggue asked. Fontenot had been at the seminar; he could have taken Dora's knife. He'd have to check on the angle of the wound.

"Was he a vengeful man, you're askin'? I guess I'd have to say so. Joseph wasn't your easy-goin' forgive-and-forget type of guy. He remembered a slight. But I wasn't thinkin' that. I was thinkin' maybe he left a note and nobody found it. Or somebody found it, but they didn't want to—''

There was a murmuring noise. Heads turned. It was almost a repeat performance of the jostling and whispering that had greeted Armand's appearance, except that this wave of movement began not at the kitchen door but at the outside door. A personage had entered.

He looked vaguely familiar to Spraggue, the way that someone seen only on television looks familiar. The man was heavy, almost wider than he was tall. He had a sallow complexion, startled blue eyes, a tiny childish nose, and wispy brown hair, parted low on the left side and brushed over a balding scalp. Some TV-critic galloping gourmet clone. Hampton something. He was coming their way, beaming a television smile. His teeth were fine.

Mary said, "Oh, here he is. I invited Harris Hampton to join us—''

It was the look on Armand's face that stopped her. The restaurant owner was out of his chair in a flash, jarring his coffee. He waited until the fat man was close enough to hear a whisper, then bellowed, "Get out!"

The man froze in his tracks. Diners paused, forks in midair.

Armand lowered his voice, but his fury was visible. "Go on. Get out!"

Mary stood, tiny beside Armand. "I'm sorry," she said, bewildered. "I had no idea—"

"You couldn't have known." Armand absolved Mary with a wave of his hand. "But this phony, this recipe thief, this hausfrau's helper, he knows he's never to enter any restaurant of mine."

"Not even—" Mary began.

"I'm sorry," Armand said, with hauteur that would have done credit to an emperor. "My decision is absolute. Thomas!"—this to the headwaiter—"show this person out."

As he watched the scene, Spraggue thought Fontenot wasn't the only chef around who held a grudge.

Aunt Mary said, "Please, Mr. Hampton, if you could stop by my hotel—in half an hour, perhaps. The Imperial Orleans. I'd like to buy you a drink . . ."

There was nothing Harris Hampton could do but nod and make as dignified a retreat as his red cheeks and waddling derriere would allow.

"I'm sorry," Mary ventured again, when the diners had gone back to their food and the buzz of whispered conversation had died.

Armand righted his coffee cup and nodded for a waiter to place a clean napkin over the offending brown stain on the tablecloth. "That man! It was pure mischief that made Denise seat him with Joe and me that night. She knew."

"Knew what?"

"How much I hate that man. But Denise Michel, well, she hates *all* men, and maybe it seemed damned funny to her, putting us together and waiting for the sparks to fly. There's a devil in that Denise."

"But surely—" Mary began soothingly.

"You want yourselves a murderer?" Armand said. "Well, there he goes. 'Murderer' is a gentle word, a kind word for a man who would publish a recipe, call it mine,

68

from my restaurant, cooked by the great Fontenot, and call for margarine in the preparation! Margarine!''

Spraggue kept his eyes averted from Mary's. He knew he would laugh if she did, knew she was about to burst.

"I mean, who is that man? Who does he think he is? An upstart nothing, that's who. No credentials. Cooks from a can. Even his name is a phony. Sticks out a mile. Made up for a newspaper column. Where's he from? What's he know about anything?'' Armand took a long sip of coffee, a deep breath, and continued in a lower tone. "I tell you, if Harris Hampton had been killed that evening, I would take the credit myself. I'd have to stand in a long line at the police station, understand, all full of cooks boastin' that they'd done a great service to the culinary world. It would have been justifiable homicide.''

"Did Joe Fontenot feel the way you do about Harris Hampton?'' Spraggue asked.

"It was his perch and redfish coo-bee-yon that Hampton ruined, publishin' that fake garbage. Fontenot hated the man.''

Coo-bee-yon? Spraggue glanced at Mary, and she whispered *"Courtbouillon"* so faintly it just reached his ears.

Spraggue said, "You think Joe might have tried to avenge his stolen recipe?''

"I think that if the two of them had a fight, Hampton and Fontenot, it would have been one hell of a screaming match right at the table. But Joe was on his best behavior that night, for the judges.''

Mary raised her eyebrows, and Spraggue understood that she had a low opinion of Fontenot's best behavior.

"No," Armand said, "much as I would love to think of Hampton in prison, cooking slop for prisoners for the rest of his life, I don't think he would have had the nerve to attack Joseph all alone, away from the crowd.''

"But suppose they met in the display room, suppose Fontenot threatened Hampton—'' Mary began.

"Well now,'' Armand said. "That's not bad. Not bad

at all. Maybe that could get your cook out of jail. Because if Joe accosted that fool, if they had a brawl, then the only way Harris Hampton would have come out on top would have been to use a knife. And plenty quick, too. But . . .''

"But?"

"Well, it sounds strange, I know, but the more I think about it, the more likely it seems that nobody killed Joe Fontenot.''

Eight

The lamplit French Quarter streets were filled with tight knots of revelers toting paper cups of booze from bar to bar. They strolled nonchalantly in front of the cab, invincible inebriates, slowing progress to a crawl. Early drunks sagged against lamp posts. The crush thinned out toward the back of the Quarter.

Albert Flowers parked the Oldsmobile three-quarters of the way up onto the sidewalk—the "banquette," he called it—and pointed across the street. Spraggue read the sign over the red door: WITCHCRAFT. A wooden board affixed to the doorjamb listed services: GOOD LUCK CHARMS, RITUAL ALTARS, SACRED SEALS, HEXES REMOVED, TALISMANS, CONSULTATIONS.

"We may be too late," Spraggue said. "The lights are off."

"They can't do that," Flowers protested. "We got an appointment. Let's bang the door down."

Spraggue knocked. Nothing. He leaned his forehead against one of the grimy windows off to the side, peered in. Way at the back of the shop he could see two flickering

71

eyes of light. One detached itself from the other and danced toward the door.

Candles, he thought. The stage is set.

The woman who opened the door, lit taper in hand, wore shoes soft enough to make no noise on the wide wooden floorboards. She was dark-skinned, plump, exotic, with sharply inverted Vs for eyebrows, so thin and precise they must have been painted on her forehead. A parrot-green scarf was wrapped around her head. Her dress was bright, layered color, long and flowing to the ground.

"You Mistah Spraggue?" she said with a touch of clipped island tang in her deep voice.

"Yes. And this is Mr. Flowers."

"You both want reading?"

"Just me."

"Then your friend wait outside. His aura disturb the reading."

"I don't like that much," Flowers interjected.

"He could wait in the shop," the woman offered. "I do reading in the back room."

"Sounds okay," Spraggue said.

Flowers nodded.

The woman opened the door wide and motioned them in with her candle.

The shop was crowded, with things not people, dark and mysteriously fragrant. The woman floated silently around the room, touching her flame to various candles, illuminating a wall covered with eerily staring masks and bookcases stuffed with old battered volumes held in place by Nefertiti bookends. The floor sloped gently downward toward a heavy desk burdened with more fat books and a brazier puffing out perfumed smoke. Shelves and counters were jammed with candles, dolls, jars and bottles of herbs: stinkwort, buckthorn, bloodroot, orris powder, black mustard seed, rue, yarrow, Dittany of Crete. One bottle was labeled "Graveyard Dirt."

"Here's some gris-gris," Flowers said, motioning Spraggue over to a central counter.

They were disappointing, just three-inch squares of colored flannel that had been tied into tiny balls with stingy ropes of yarn and tossed in a basket in a jumble of different colors. Spraggue smelled a white one and found it sweet and pungent. Herbs, seeds, roots, maybe. There was a sign over the basket:

> *Gris-Gris*
> *black—cursing*
> *white—protection & purity*
> *gold—money*
> *blue—love*

They didn't look anything like the leather pouch Mary had lifted from Sergeant Rawlins' desk drawer, the pouch now in Spraggue's pocket.

"These just tourist trash," Flowers whispered. "No harm in 'em though. You gonna dig up nasty things for the police, maybe you should get one of them white ones."

"Maybe one of each," Spraggue said.

The woman motioned Flowers to a chair, and handed him a stack of books to browse through. Her movements were economical. She spoke only when necessary, using one bare arm, one tiny hand with long red-painted talons, for soundless gestures. When Flowers was situated, she led Spraggue through a curtained archway into another room.

The walls were black, covered with some sort of material that absorbed the light and made dimensions difficult to ascertain. An oil lamp sat in the middle of a round table covered with a black cloth. As they entered the circle of muted lamplight, the woman blew out her candle with a hissing drawn-out exhalation.

The room reeked of spices and herbs. Incense. She said, "You can call me Sister Delores."

"Thank you," Spraggue replied gravely.

She fiddled with something at the base of the lamp and the circle of light grew. The table was in the center of a pentagram taped onto the wooden floorboards with wide gaffer's tape. Sister Delores took a candle from the table, muttered at it, set it aflame, then placed it in a holder on a small high platform against the far wall.

Candlelight transformed the platform into an altar. Against the wall, a brass cross. Before it, a figure that could have been the Virgin Mary, or Mother Nature, stood on a scrap of blue satin. A Bible was open in front of the figure. Two statues flanked the book, but Spraggue couldn't identify them. A brass bell sat to the left of the Bible, the candlestick to the right.

"Enter the holy configuration," said Sister Delores, "and sit you down." She raised her hand and touched cool fingertips to his forehead. "These creases speak to me of troubles, mistah. You look like a man with troubles."

Spraggue sank into a metal chair. It tilted under his weight; one leg was shorter than the others.

"If the good luck evades you, mistah, I make you a charm. Many herbs here with healing powers. Loadstone, John the Conqueror Root, Devil's Shoe String Root. Put those in conjunction with a bit of Adam Root, a bit of Eve Root, in the right time, in the right way, they bring back your luck."

"What about a gris-gris?" Spraggue asked.

"Gris-gris? That a fine charm, a hoodoo bag. Some call them mojo, some wanga. You want a gris-gris to change your luck?"

"I already have a gris-gris. It was given to me. And I wonder if maybe it's the wrong kind, if it's putting bad luck on me instead of good luck."

"You get it from a practitioner? Somebody who knows this stuff? Plenty bad practitioners. Don't know roots from herbs."

Spraggue drew the leather pouch from his pocket. "Can you tell me what this charm does? Who made it?"

"Put it on the table, man. I don't want touch it yet. You think this be giving you bad luck? You think you got a curse on you?"

"I don't know," Spraggue said. "I was hoping you'd tell me."

"This ain't what I do, for a psychic reading."

"I know. But my friend said you were a very powerful practitioner. He thought you might be able to tell me things others wouldn't know. I would make it worth your while."

Sister Delores settled back in her chair, a faint smile on her placid face. "First, you tell me about who gave you this gris-gris."

"It's a little complicated. The man is dead."

"Good." She nodded her head several times, her expression fixed. "It's important you tell me this. You handle the property of dead men different than you handle the property of men still alive." Sheathing one hand in a fold of her dress she moved the gris-gris bag closer to her. "No smell of the graveyard," she said. "Still, I think if it belong to your dead man, it was taken from him after his death. He die by violence?"

"Yes," Spraggue said. Her voice was hypnotic. He wondered if the herb incense was fogging his brain.

"You want to know how he died?"

"I already know that. He was stabbed."

"Then you want to know who kill him?"

"Yes. I would. Very much."

"I can't tell you that." Sister Delores leaned back in her chair, her hands spread flat on the tablecloth. "I can tell you a way to find out."

"What's that?"

"Very old voodoo wanga. They use it in New Orleans long ago. I tell it to you. Let me remember." She closed her eyes and hummed a single plaintive note. "You break an egg, a fresh egg, in the palm of your dead man's right hand, see? Then you bury him just the same you bury anybody die peaceful in their bed. But on top of the freshly turned earth in the center of the grave, you put the egg-shell. Then the killer he come and seek you out. He tell you everything. He confess his sins. This happen either in seven hours or in seven days. Very old wanga and good one, too."

Not the slightest hint of a smile lightened the woman's voice or demeanor. Spraggue stared at her eyes, trying to guess her age. Thirty to fifty. Ageless. Young skin and old eyes.

Spraggue wondered how the coroner would react to the eggshell business, and had to bite the inside of his cheek. He said, "Could you tell me where the dead man got this gris-gris?"

"Ah." She sat still a long time, a fixed and staring statue. "I can't tell you that. Some mojo, some gris-gris, I can tell you right off who made them, who the practitioner be. But not this one. This one old."

"What can you tell me about it?"

"I have to open it up to tell you anything. Mostly I can tell a bit from the outside because gris-gris usually from cotton material, different colors. But a leather bag like this mean a fine gris-gris. Maybe your man be a practitioner himself?"

"I don't know."

She bent over the table, and after muttering something to herself, inhaled audibly, her nose barely an inch from the leather bag. "Ah," she murmured.

Spraggue raised one eyebrow.

"The smell is sweet. I will open it. If it had an evil smell I would not touch it. A gris-gris from a dead man may have caused his death, you know. But such a curse would not smell sweet."

She smiled, her teeth a flash of brilliance in the shadowy room. "I say a few words over the bag, to protect myself from evil. Mostly the power of the bag die with the owner, but I take no chances." She chanted, swaying slightly in her chair. The oil lamp's circle of light cut the table off from the rest of the room; it seemed to float in a dark pool.

Delores stood in one fluid motion, left the circle of light, and disappeared. Spraggue strained to hear faint footsteps. She was gone only an instant, then reappeared carrying a silver knife as delicate as a letter-opener and a square of red silk. The blade glinted in the lamplight as she sliced the heavy threads that bound the gris-gris. Muttering, she spread the silk on the table, dumped the leather bag's contents in the center.

A cloud of fragrant dust hit Spraggue's nostrils.

"Oh, very good," she said. "Fine. This powerful gris-gris for protection. Most powerful. This bag should protect this man."

"It didn't," Spraggue said. "What's in it?"

Her red talons pried through the pile of herbs. "John the Conqueror Root. Loadstone. A tooth, maybe from an alligator. That mighty strong luck charm. They say Marie Laveau herself wore an alligator tooth 'round her neck till she died. Plenty unusual, an alligator tooth."

"Expensive?"

"You bet. Plenty expensive. Leather bag. Alligator tooth. I think this man knows who his enemy is and has this made special, a long time ago."

"How old would you say it is?"

"Oh, very old. This a man with a longtime worry. He know somebody's after him and he go to a practitioner and he tell her and she make him a powerful charm. Or maybe he try something very dangerous and he know he need big help. Maybe he be going off to war and he be afraid he won't come back. This man owned this gris-gris, he one worried man."

"Sounds serious," Spraggue murmured.

"Oh, man," Sister Delores said earnestly, "don't underestimate the power. This serious protection, this charm. This belong to a man afraid of death."

"Aren't we all?"

"Not like this, mistah. The man owns this gris-gris afraid of special kind of death. Early death. Unnatural death. Like he got."

Nine

"**S**he say you gonna meet a dark-haired beautiful woman?" Albert Flowers asked as Spraggue emerged from the back room of the witchcraft shop.

"Is that the usual spiel?"

"Nope. But meetin' a fine-lookin' woman is what you're gonna do. It's early yet, but not too soon to start bar-hoppin'."

"Sorry—" Spraggue started to say.

Flowers halted his protest with an upraised hand. "And Fontenot's daughter," he said pointedly, "she start work at ten. Second shift."

"Sorry." The word was the same but Spraggue's intonation took a hundred-and-eighty-degree spin. "Where does she work?"

"Place on Bourbon. Not one of your more refined ones, neither. Crummy kind of joint. Strippers. Boys and girls. I don't think she takes her clothes off, but she's probably a semi-pro, if you know what I mean. She's a waitress there."

"Not someplace Daddy would approve of."

Flowers grinned. "Depends on what kinda Daddy she got."

Abandoning the cab, they strolled up Bourbon Street. The humid night air, just breezy enough to warrant his tweed sports jacket, made Spraggue wonder what streak of masochism had kept him North so many winters.

While they walked Flowers spun the tale of his pursuit of Mrs. Fontenot's daughter, of her dauntless green VW Rabbit, and her atrocious driving habits.

"I'll stick with you in the bar until I can point her out," he said. "Then—"

"Then you call it a night. You do good work."

"Thanks."

The flashing neon sign out front said *The Creole Strip.* The place was tiny, a narrow alley tarted up for Mardi Gras. Gaudy striped bunting, purple, yellow, and green, creased from storage and spotted with beer, hung limply from the scratched imitation-walnut bar. The lighting was erratic—dim at the bar so the patrons wouldn't realize how much water was mixed with the booze, glaring near the elevated plank stage, bright enough to count the freckles blotching the chest of the impersonally naked woman who wriggled and sweated under the searching spotlight. Two hugely muscled bouncers flanked the stage and kept the men who nursed their watered drinks from leaping up onto the platform and counting the dancer's freckles with their fingertips.

Spraggue and Flowers ordered drinks at the bar. It took the cabbie about the same time to locate Fontenot's daughter as it took the bartender to fetch two pale Scotches.

"There," Flowers said softly. "She's that dark-haired lady in the shiny red shirt. I'm gonna stay here till she gets close to us, and you drink your stuff fast. When I get offa the stool, if I time it right, she'll climb aboard and try to get you to take a table and stand her some champagne. It ain't your pretty face. That's what these chickies are paid to do. It'll cost ya."

Spraggue nodded and drank. The stuff was terrible. He turned to stare at the swaying woman on the stage. Framed in the dirty mirror over the bar, his profile was strong-jawed, the nose long, thin, and faintly crooked, the forehead high. His profile was his best angle, the one resume photographers chose. It disguised the asymmetrical features that made his face "interesting" rather than "handsome," kept him a "character actor" instead of a "leading man."

Flowers managed his exit with the grace of a Bolshoi principal.

The dark-haired woman slipped onto the barstool with an aggressive display of leg. She wasn't much more than a girl, maybe eighteen, maybe less. She didn't look anything like her mother. Jeannine Fontenot worked to make herself attractive. The younger woman had beauty in spite of herself. Nature, not the cosmetic industry, had shadowed her dark smudgy eyes. Her high cheekbones were innocent of powder or rouge. She was striking, possessing an off-beat, quiet kind of beauty that was more attractive because it wasn't on public display. It left you wondering if you were the only one who had noticed it.

She lifted a cigarette to her mouth and tilted her head in his direction, waiting for a light. It was such a practiced, mechanized come-on that Spraggue wondered whether she had to get herself doped up before heading for work.

"Hi," he said faintly, scrambling for a matchbook and deciding that the wariness of the traveling businessman, with a pocket full of credit cards and a wife safely in Dubuque, was called for.

She raised the heat of a calculated smile an eighth of a degree. "You can hardly see from here," she said. "This isn't the best seat in the house."

"Crowded," he mumbled, looking a little embarrassed. What would they say in Dubuque about him being in a strip joint? "I just came in to look around."

The smile got warmer. "If you wanted to do some serious drinking, say a bottle, I could get us a table down front. Claudine's dancing now and she's not bad, but Annette, the woman who'll be on in fifteen minutes, she is totally hot, and she really can dance, if you like that sort of stuff.''

"Uh . . .'' Spraggue said. Dubuque would think it over.

"I'm Aimee. Spelled French, with two *e*'s.''

"You work here?''

"Sort of.'' She licked her bottom lip in a gesture that was a parody of all the come-ons in all the B-movies he'd ever seen.

"I see,'' he said, and his voice matched her licked lips, saying more than his words.

"I sort of have an arrangement with the management,'' she went on. "Want that table?''

"Sure,'' he said bravely, recklessly. "Why not?'' A sucker performance. Well and truly hooked.

Her smile was different this time, tinged with scorn and a certain amount of relief. She led the way to a table not much bigger than an oil drum that was filled with dirty bar glasses and wadded napkins. The music pulsed in his right ear, wailing rock and roll by Tina Turner. Claudine lifted her arms high over her head and shook her heavy breasts.

"Is Aimee your real name or, uh, your stage name?'' Spraggue asked. He moved his chair closer to Aimee's, leaned forward and spoke in her ear. It was the only way to be heard over the blaring music. He didn't mind. In the stink of spilled beer and tobacco smoke, her hair smelled unexpectedly sweet.

She let her eyelashes drop demurely. "You mean do I, uh . . .'' She flicked a nod in Claudine's direction. "No. I don't dance, here.'' Her voice left open the possibility that she gave private performances, maybe even lessons.

Spraggue let his eyes slide down the V of her shiny red blouse. It was cut deep both front and back and only good posture seemed to keep the sleeves on her shoulders. There was a tracing of white lace ornamenting the curve of her

82

breasts. A camisole, probably. Too much action when she walked for a bra.

He said, a little husky-voiced, "You could dance in better places than this." By this time Dubuque would be moist-palmed and breathing hard. "With your looks, I mean," he stammered on, "uh, if you've got the moves." He felt his face redden as he spoke. Actor's tricks.

"You're cute," she said, squeezing his hand and smiling with bored eyes. "Aimee's my real true name. A good Cajun name. Right from the bayou to New Orleans." She pronounced it "N'Awlins."

Champagne came, New York State at Dom Perignon prices. Hick champagne and squat flat glasses. They clicked glasses before drinking.

"Uh, you work here long?" Spraggue shouted in her ear, when the silent eyeplay had gone on long enough. Her knee made contact with his right leg. She leaned closer as he spoke to her. Definitely a camisole.

She had the good sense to look offended at his question. "Hell, no," she said. "I'm here part-time, helping out a friend. I'm a student, really. I take classes at Tulane."

Flowers hadn't mentioned that. Spraggue wondered if it was truth or fantasy. Made up to raise the price, maybe. To go with the unexpected vulnerability of those wide eyes, so at odds with her classic hooker ploys.

"In dance?" he asked.

"Anthropology," she said abruptly, shutting down that avenue of discussion. "Now tell me about you. You haven't even told me your name and you know all about me." Her face settled into a frozen mask of rapt attention. Her eyes died. Time for the John to talk about himself. Tune out.

Without thinking, he gave his understudy's name at the Harvard Rep. "Jonah Turner, from, uh, Dubuque. Plumbing supplies." Spraggue realized that he'd been doing Jonah all along. The flat Midwestern accent. The earnest, embarrassed blushes. Dubuque, that's where Jonah hailed from.

Plumbing supplies—with better sense that's what Jonah would have gone into.

"And you're here for a convention," Aimee said, pressing closer.

"How'd you guess?"

"You look like a businessman."

Spraggue swallowed the blow to his self-esteem. "Your last name as pretty as your first, Aimee?" He'd better start getting some information out of her and stop putting himself into Jonah Turner's character, because Jonah Turner would have just tried to get the girl out of there fast, back to some hotel. He wouldn't have worried about the fact that she was young enough to be his daughter, and probably underage.

"Aimee Fontenot," she said.

"And that's your real name?" He made it sound as if he knew she was putting him on.

"A lot of the, uh, dancers, here don't go by their real names. You know, in case Momma or Daddy find out. Me, I don't care. I'd use my own name even if I stripped."

"You that proud of it? Or you want to hurt somebody?" The comment was out of character for Jonah Turner. Spraggue hoped she'd drunk enough not to notice.

"Nobody left to hurt," she muttered. "Come on. Drink up. Champagne's getting warm." She touched her glass to her lips, but barely sipped at it. He didn't blame her.

"You gotta boyfriend, or a husband, or something?" Spraggue said, draining his glass and looking around warily. Dubuque was panicking a little.

"What makes you think that?"

"What you said. About nobody left to hurt. I mean if you were using your husband's name, like, to, uh, dance under, I bet it would piss him off good. And I don't want to—"

"Relax," she said. "No husband."

"Than who's not left to hurt?"

84

He waited for the ''none of your business'' his query deserved. But he didn't get it.

''My old man, my father, died.''

''Hey, I'm sorry,'' Spraggue said, taking her hand and giving her that special, sincere actor-look that Jonah did so well. On stage it wasn't bad. In real life, it always made him want to puke.

''You don't have to be.'' She started to shake off his hand, but then she must have remembered her job. She ran her fingers lightly over his palm.

''My dad died this past fall,'' Spraggue lied. ''I know just how you feel.'' His parents had died in a fiery car crash two days after he'd turned fourteen. It had taken the medical examiner almost a week to identify the bodies.

''No way,'' Aimee said, turning her eyes toward the stage. ''My papa and me, we had a real special relationship. I hated his guts.'' She was looking at the stage, but she was seeing something else.

''Hey, you don't want to say a thing like that,'' Spraggue said, releasing her hand as if it had given off a surge of electricity.

''Drink up,'' she said. ''Not everybody's dad is as nice as your daddy was. My papa was a louse. He got what he deserved.''

''He die badly?'' Spraggue asked. ''Cancer?''

The applause, shouts, and jeers hit a crescendo. Claudine's routine ended with a clash of cymbals. The stage lights dimmed.

''They'll take a five-minute break and then Annette'll come on,'' Aimee said. ''She'll heat the place up, I guarantee. Unless you're warm enough already?'' She reminded him of an actress doing the three-hundredth performance of the same role.

Jonah Turner would have stared down that blouse, said he was plenty hot enough and why didn't they go back to his hotel for a while? Or better still, her place, since some

85

of his co-conventioneers might lack discretion once they were back home.

Spraggue wondered if he'd get more information out of her in bed. Or forget all about information. Or get picked up for soliciting an underage hooker.

Aimee stared at him from beneath her full dark eyelashes. Spraggue took a deep breath and decided he'd better stay put.

"You know, I just read about some guy named Fontenot in the newspapers," he said.

One of her high black heels started tapping the floorboards. Her knee rubbed against Spraggue's leg, but the rhythm was angry, not seductive.

"I remember," Spraggue said. "The guy who got killed at that restaurant thing. You read about that?"

"I don't read the papers. Nothing but bad news."

"That's a good idea. Some of the news is real upsetting. Like this guy getting stabbed. I don't know why it bothered me. Maybe because I was hoping to eat at his restaurant. Maybe because he was killed on Thursday night. You know how you sometimes remember exactly what you were doing on the day somebody died?"

"No," she said bluntly.

He hoped she was still listening. He got the feeling that something deep inside her had turned completely off, that she would smile and nod no matter what he said.

He'd planned to mention the day Kennedy was shot as an example, but realized he was talking to a girl who probably hadn't been born then.

"Were you working here Thursday night?" he asked. "Or do you have a class Thursdays?"

She rested her chin on her hand and shook her head slowly. "Shit," she said finally. "I shoulda known. Momma described you to me real good. You're the man from that awful newspaper."

"No," Spraggue said. "I'm no journalist."

86

"She said you were from the *Star*. How can you work for that shit-pile paper?"

He thought it was a great comment coming from a woman typecast to be asked that deathless question, "What's a nice girl like you?" et cetera. He opened his wallet and displayed his P.I. photostat.

"Oh," she said. "I see. This must have something to do with my dear daddy's untimely death." Her tight mouth and sarcastic tone didn't express loving filial sentiment.

"It does."

"Well, get lost. Dear old daddy didn't have a lot of time for me when he was alive, and I haven't got a lot of time for him now that he's dead."

"I'm impressed," Spraggue said. "Too bad your old man isn't around to listen in."

"He was never around when I wanted him. I didn't even know I had a daddy until I was practically grown up."

"Look," Spraggue said in a conciliatory tone, "I'm sure it was hard. I'd like to hear about it."

"It's a bore. My shrink says if he'd been home when I was really little, he wouldn't have—he might have—he would have treated me more like a daughter."

"And less like a . . . ?" Spraggue prompted.

"Who are you working for? Do you have a client or are you trying to hook up to one? Because neither me or my momma is going to pay you one red cent to avenge old Joe."

"I've got a client."

"Who?"

"The woman who's in jail for killing your father."

"Yeah?"

"She didn't do it."

"Too bad."

"What?"

"I'd be a lot more sympathetic if she had."

The music revved up, louder than before. Hooting cat-calls were drowned out by shrieking brass as a Chinese woman clad in a silky, brief kimono and spiky heels tottered out to center stage.

"Maybe we could talk about this someplace else," Spraggue shouted over the cacophony.

"I'm sure we could," she said with a sweet smile. "For a price." She waved the check at him, and waited for him to put enough cash on the table to cover the tab. Then she daintily lifted two fingers to her mouth and let go with a piercing whistle. A minute earlier it wouldn't have been heard, but now it carried easily over a drumroll.

Spraggue never did get to see Annette dance.

The two lumbering bouncers knew the signal well. They lifted him out of his chair.

"I get the idea," Spraggue said.

Two hundred pounds of muscle latched on to each of his arms.

"Hey," he said. "I can walk."

They heaved him out the front door. He missed hitting a Lucky Dog hot dog vendor by a good inch, then staggered into a crowd of Bourbon Street drunks. Half of them cursed; half of them didn't even notice.

Ten

The door to the suite swung open before Spraggue could finish fishing the key out of his pocket. Pierce bobbed his head in formal greeting, then winked to undermine the formality. The spine of the Spraggue mansion staff since time immemorial, Pierce had streaks of gray icing his shiny black hair, and a hairline that was rapidly retreating from shaggy eyebrows. Tall and spare, almost grim, he had the underappreciated ability to fade into the background. Pierce rarely called Spraggue by name anymore. He thought "Michael" too familiar, in spite of Spraggue's insistence, and sometimes fell back on the "Master Mike" of twenty years ago.

"Your aunt is—" Pierce began, taking no apparent notice of Spraggue's rumpled appearance.

"Darling," Mary's voice fluted through the archway. "Do join us."

"Company?" Spraggue murmured.

"Denise Michel," Pierce whispered. "The cookbook lady. Formidable! And a friend of hers." Pierce hesitated a second before choosing the word "friend," but his face, as usual, gave nothing away.

So much for a long hot bath laced with the baking soda he'd picked up at the all-night drugstore. Soaks the stiffness right out, a stage-fighting instructor had once enthused while discussing cures for muscles stretched in pursuit of the perfect fencing-match riposte. Not panaceas for barroom brawls. Spraggue shrugged, and then regretted the movement. The bouncers had been brusque and professional. No arguments brooked, no bones broken. His left shoulder protested when he tossed his jacket on the sofa.

"And," Pierce added, "we bailed Dora out."

"She's here?"

The butler nodded. "Sleeping. An adjoining room."

Spraggue followed his aunt's voice into the dining nook and found her presiding over the ruins of a banquet. A rich, spicy smell pervaded the room. The table, its length extended by a room service cart, had been swathed in a white linen cloth. Elaborate place settings—two wineglasses apiece and a flotilla of silverware—were scattered in disarray. Brown sauce congealed on the dinner plates. A half-full wine bottle kept two empty ones company in the center of the table.

A gaunt older woman, her long face full of harsh lines that gave it character, sat at his aunt's right. She was wearing beige slacks and a shapeless checked shirt. Her shoulders would have done credit to a fullback. On Mary's left sat another woman, this one young and pallidly pretty, in a sprigged cotton dress of Victorian cut.

Denise Michel, the older woman, offered a no-nonsense jerk of her head and a firm handshake. Paulette Thibideaux, the younger, blushed.

"We have had the most marvelous meal," Mary said, beaming. "Barbequed oysters, chicken Pontalba—"

"Nothing so special." Denise Michel ducked her head in what looked like honest embarrassment. Her cheeks were flushed. "Paulette did the oysters very well, I thought." She had a rough croaking voice, with a slight French lilt, that Spraggue found attractive.

The young woman blushed again. Spraggue wondered if she did anything else besides cook and blush. Speak, for instance.

"You're a cook here?" Spraggue asked the question mainly to test her vocal capabilities, although he was puzzled by her presence at the table.

"Only a waitress really." Her voice was both reedy and nasal. With that voice, a blush sufficed. "On the banquet staff. But Denise—Miss Michel—is teaching me to cook." There was hero worship in her glance, that and a little more.

"Denise was just telling me about Henri Fiorici," Mary said, slurring her words. Her gentle smile included everyone in the room, inviting them all to join her as she raised her wineglass to her lips.

Two and a half bottles of wine for three people. Mary's tipsiness had to be an act. She was the world bantamweight drinking champion. Spraggue watched as his aunt, her hand steady as a rock, unobtrusively refilled first Denise Michel's glass, then Paulette's.

Denise Michel outweighed Mary by fifty pounds. By virtue of sheer size, she should have been able to handle a bottle or two without risk of indiscretion, should have been able to drink tiny Mary under any table. But Denise was the one with the flushed cheeks. And fragile Paulette seemed to be having trouble sitting up straight.

"To Henri." Denise lifted her glass in a toast, and Paulette solemnly echoed her motion. "Again, he takes off at the first sign of trouble. Just like the old days . . ."

"The old days?" Spraggue repeated.

"He is gone. Already. He flew yesterday back to New York. Never any guts. I tell that to Dora, way back."

"Dora worked at Fiorici's restaurant in New York, after she left New Orleans." Mary's quiet response to Spraggue's lifted eyebrow came quickly enough to prove her sobriety.

"Did the police say Fiorici could leave town?" Spraggue aimed the question at his aunt, but Denise intercepted it.

"But certainly. Why not? They think they have the killer dead to rights. How was I to—?" She stopped abruptly. "Sit down," she said to Spraggue. "Why do you stand? Paulette fetch another wineglass off the tray. Or give him one of yours. You drink?"

Spraggue's liking for Denise Michel increased. "You bet," he said. The white burgundy would rinse the bar champagne off his tongue.

Denise poured. Her hand was huge and gnarled, the wrist as big as any man's. "I have been gossiping with your aunt," she said, and let an unexpected giggle escape.

Not quite drunk, Spraggue thought, but with a definite buzz on, a pre-drunk glow.

"Anyway," she continued, "it was long ago. It no longer matters. Every week Henri Fiorici would beg Dora to marry him. Every Sunday when he got back from Mass, she told me. After confession, he had more courage."

"Is that why you invited him to the Great Chef's banquet?" Spraggue asked. "Because he used to know Dora?"

"Me? I did not invite him." The idea upset Denise Michel. "He is a member. Yes, it's true, I arranged that he should sit with us. But I was not responsible for the invitations—"

"Except for Dora's," Spraggue said.

"She, too, is a member."

"But she'd never have come if you hadn't seconded the formal invitation with a personal plea," Spraggue said. "Isn't that true?"

"Perhaps. Believe me, if I had for one moment thought, if I had known—" Denise opened, then shut her mouth, pressing her lips together in a frown.

Not drunk enough. "Known what?" Spraggue asked.

"That Fontenot would get himself killed, of course. What else? That the imbecile police would arrest the wrong person. Out of all the host who hated Fontenot, how could they be so stupid as to arrest Dora? The logic, you understand, it escapes me.''

"Denise did not care for Mr. Fontenot," Mary said quietly. "As a chef."

"A chef!" Denise made a squawking noise and flung her arms wide, barely missing a wine bottle. "A short-order cook! Or rather a long-order cook, always simmering pots full of slop. What did the man do? Peasant food. Soup and stew. Cheap messes with no delicacy, no refinement. The man knew nothing about food, nothing! He had no training, only a big mouth. And he fooled everyone."

"Not everyone," Paulette said loyally.

"I'm sorry." Denise smiled at the younger woman. "I get carried away, you can see. Cooking is passionate business. And that Fontenot, he made everything crazy." She turned her attention to Spragague; he was a new audience for a well-rehearsed scene. "Here we have Creole food, which is in the grand French tradition, and Cajun food, which is also good, but which is truly peasant food. To open a gourmet Cajun restaurant—*mon dieu!*—it is the same thing as to open a fancy-dress McDonald's with marble arches!"

"Absolutely!" Paulette shook her head vigorously in agreement, like a spaniel wagging its tail.

"Eh, bien!" Denise threw up her hands, ruffled her short graying hair. "Why do I go on like this, fighting with a dead man, eh? It is only that he infuriated me so. Do you know what this man did? Do you know? I write cookbooks. Good cookbooks, and this man was jealous. He went to my publisher, and he said that he would do a better cookbook than me."

Denise Michel leaned back and folded her arms, leaving her listeners to appreciate the utter absurdity of Fontenot's claim.

"Is cookbook writing also passionate business?" Spragague inquired. "Like cooking?"

"For me, it is money business. For others?" She

shrugged her massive shoulders. "It is fortunate I have an ironclad contract with my publisher, yes?"

Did she? "Miss Michel—" Spraggue began.

"Denise," she corrected.

"Denise." He repeated it as she had said it: Denize. "When did you realize that Joseph Fontenot was the man who had married Dora under another name?"

The creases across her forehead deepened. "It is hard to say, *monsieur*. There's such a separation in time, you see. One does not think about them together. Dora cooks in New Orleans in, oh, the early sixties. Fontenot, I never hear of until, eh, maybe 'seventy-seven, 'seventy-eight. And then I do not meet him. He is only a name, a man who cooks pretentious Cajun food. But then, we are thrown together this past month. I have met him before, but never for more than a passing moment. Both of us are on the committee to arrange the Great Chefs' meeting. I am honored to have them come to my hotel. Always I have looked forward to being the hostess of such a dinner, with fine food and fine wine, and people who appreciate fine food and fine wine. And even that, this Fontenot spoils—"

"Why tell the police," Spraggue said slowly, "about Dora and the dead man. She was your friend—"

Paulette got defensive. "What else could she do? There was the man, dead on the floor—"

"Calm yourself, Paulette." Denise spoke as if to a child. "I can speak for myself, *chérie. Monsieur*, listen to me. I tell the police only the truth. All my life I have read crime stories, mostly French ones. *Romans policiers.* And always someone does not tell the truth. And always, it would have been better if they had. I do not believe that my old friend killed this Fontenot. He was a man well hated, a man waiting to be killed."

"You can tell the truth," Spraggue said, "and still hold something back."

There was a sharp knock on the door. Spraggue looked at his aunt, but she shrugged her ignorance.

"We must go." Denise Michel stood and Spraggue was awed by her height. The massive shoulders were in proportion to the rest of her. The mousey Paulette was dwarfed as she rose unsteadily to her feet.

"One more thing," Spraggue said quickly. "During the banquet, did you leave the room? Go to the kitchen to check on things?"

"The kitchen here is well run by my staff. I have no need to race back and forth and attend to every detail myself."

Pierce loomed in the archway. "Detective Sergeant Rawlins to see you."

It was Paulette who whirled at Pierce's voice, upsetting her wineglass. In a flurry of awkward actions, she blushed, stammered an apology, and gazed up at Denise like a spaniel about to be whipped. Her napkin staunched the stream of pale wine.

Spraggue asked, "Which table did you wait on that night, Miss Thibideaux?"

"Oh, please," she said, "I'm not usually so clumsy. I didn't—"

"No. I'm not accusing you of spilling anything. I just wanted to know if you'd noticed Fontenot that night."

Denise said, "Shall I send you up another bottle of wine?"

Mary nodded gravely. She looked entirely sober now. She could probably play back the entire dinner conversation with the accuracy of a tape recorder.

The interruption gave Paulette a chance to regroup. She clung to the back of her chair. "I waited at the head table, *monsieur*," she said, borrowing a little of Denise's French lilt. "Where the judges sat. It was an honor for me. I don't recall seeing Monsieur Fontenot."

Denise bowed her way out, Paulette mimicking her ungainly stride. Spraggue drained his glass and set it back in the forest of glassware on the table. His right bicep felt like it had been squeezed in a vise.

"Interesting," Spraggue said.

"What?" Mary was surveying the wreckage of the tablecloth. Breadcrumbs, wine stains, spilled coffee. "Let's go into the study."

"Are you drunk?"

"Me?" Mary drew herself up with dignity. "Mainly, I poured. A waste of good wine."

"Just who is little Paulette?"

"Denise knows her mother. She's taken a special interest in her. In training her to cook. That's what she said, at any rate."

"Paulette brought up the food?"

"Yes. Cook, waitress, and unexpected guest. Denise will probably send someone else to handle the clean-up. Paulette doesn't handle her drinking well."

"But she seems devoted to Denise," Spraggue added thoughtfully. "Denise invited her to join your little party."

"Yes. And I agreed, because she was a waitress at the banquet. What about it?"

"I don't know." Spraggue shook his head to clear the fog of Scotch, champagne, and burgundy. "Something about the way Paulette looked at Denise, it bothered me. Sometimes she looked like a worshipper at an altar. And sometimes . . ."

"Yes?"

"Sometimes she looked like the sacrifice."

Eleven

Sergeant Rawlins looked thinner than he had at the station. His navy suit camouflaged his stomach. His jawline showed the evidence of a hasty shave. He'd even made an effort to slick back the cloud of white hair. When Mary offered her hand, he leaned over and brushed it with his lips.

Spraggue wondered if he ought to get lost.

Mary said, "You look like a man bearing good news."

"You didn't tell me she was a mind reader." Rawlins flashed a sidelong grin at Spraggue.

"Only when the moon's full," he replied.

Mary shrugged. "The rest of the time, I'm reduced to reading tea leaves. Have you got something?"

"Have I got somethin'?" Rawlins patted the pockets of his suit until one of them yielded a folded sheet of paper. "Set yourselves down and take a peek at this. I only made the one copy, so's you'll have to share."

MURDER IN MORGAN CITY screamed the headline.

"Huh?" Spraggue unfolded the paper. It was legal-size, cheap and white, fresh from a Xerox machine. Either the original clipping had been in bad shape or the copier needed service. "Where's Morgan City?"

"Read first, questions later." Rawl sat in the only chair designed for his weight, folded his hands over his paunch, and turned into a smiling Buddha. Mary and Spraggue huddled on the couch, heads bent close together.

> In a mid-morning attack on an armored car carrying the payrolls of several major oil drilling companies, one guard was killed, one severely wounded, and a third man, allegedly one of the robbers, was shot and later apprehended by the Morgan City Police. Estimates of the loss range from $150,000 to well over $1,000,000.

"What's this got to do with—" Mary began.
"Read," Rawlins replied sternly.

> Lieutenant Gil Dumais of the Morgan City Police stated that three masked assailants were involved in the well-planned robbery, two armed with handguns, one with an automatic weapon. Two of the suspects escaped and are the object of an intensive police search.
>
> The wounded were taken to Sisters of Mercy hospital, where the name of the injured guard was not immediately available. The dead guard's name is being withheld pending notification of next of kin. Both were employees of Southeast Security, Inc. The name of the wounded suspect, now under guard at Sisters of Mercy, is given as James French, age and address unknown.

There was a date handscrawled on the corner. Spraggue thought it might be September, '66. He glanced questioningly up at Rawlins.

"Wait till your aunt's done readin'."

Mary sighed. "If this is supposed to make lightbulbs appear over my head, I'm afraid I may disappoint you."

Rawlins leaned forward and rubbed his palms together in anticipation. "Lookit, your nephew said somethin' to me this afternoon, about checkin' out the dead man, 'cause he married your cook usin' an alias. I wouldn't have even tried fingerprints, except we got this fancy computer scanner system on loan from the Feds. Japanese make it. NEC. Costs enough to pay five hundred extra beat officers or somethin', so I'm bettin' we never buy one, but I sure am gonna stick in a good word for that machine after this. Checks six hundred and fifty file prints per second! Picked those prints out so fast my head's still spinnin'. Woulda taken a good print man thirty years. If he got lucky."

"Sergeant Rawlins—" Mary began.

"Hey," Rawlins said reproachfully, "I thought we agreed on 'Rawl.' "

"Rawl, I'm not understanding this. What's an old robbery got to do with fingerprints?"

Rawlins turned to Spraggue. "You talk to Jeannine Fontenot this morning? She say her old man spent some years away from her?"

Had Rawlins had him followed? Was there a fine for impersonating a trashy journalist? "She said he spent time in France, learning to cook."

"France, huh?" Rawlins leaned back, a grin splitting his plump face. "Angola's pretty damn far from France."

"Angola?" Mary said. "As in African Angola?"

"Angola as in Louisiana," Rawlins announced. "Site of Louisiana State Prison."

Spraggue broke the silence with a low whistle.

"What I mean is," the sergeant continued, pleased with the reaction, "this guy who got arrested for robbin' the payroll in Morgan City, back in 'sixty-six, under the name of James French, keeps the same damn prints on the ends of his fingers as Joe Fontenot. We're not lookin' at a dead man who changed his name once for the purpose of connin' some poor lady into matrimony. We're starin' at a six-year jail term and multiple aliases."

"James French," Spraggue repeated. "And when he married Dora, he was Jacques Forte." He ticked off the names on his fingers. "When he married Jeannine, he was Joe Fontenot. Must have had monogrammed underwear."

"Rawl," Mary said, "this is wonderful!"

The detective's fat cheeks reddened.

"Is there more?" Spraggue asked.

"Well." Rawlins stretched out the syllable, while he patted down his pockets again, then removed a tiny notebook. "I got a few things jotted down. Got a guy on the way over to Morgan City right now." Rawlins thumbed through the pages, held the notebook open at arm's length, moved it slowly closer.

"Rawl," Mary murmured.

"Okay, okay," he muttered, reaching into his breast pocket, yanking out a leather case. "I'm not tryin' to hold back." Reluctantly, he perched a pair of reading glasses on the bridge of his nose. They were thin rectangular slits, framed in black. "I want to say it all at once, and I don't know right where to start. I might just head up to Angola to talk to the warden tomorrow—"

Pierce had an entire vocabulary of door knocks. This one was subdued, perfunctory—an announcement of interruption rather than a request to enter. He presented a bottle on a silver tray.

Mary accepted the accompanying white and silver card, while Spraggue read the label on the bottle. "Compliments of the hotel," she announced. "That means Denise."

"Cognac," Spraggue said. "A Sabourin Grande Champagne. A major league bribe." He wondered about Paulette, about the possibility of linked murderers, one with motive, the other with opportunity.

"Pour us each a glass, Pierce," Mary said, "yourself included—and we'll drink to this marvelous policeman."

The praise made Rawlins sit taller in his chair. "James French," he said, consulting first the notebook, then the folded sheet of paper, reading easily now with the aid of the despised glasses, "also known as Joe Fontenot. What he served time for in Angola was quite some rumpus, back in 1966." Rawlins clamped the notebook shut, using his index finger for a marker, and lifted off his glasses. They left shallow red tracks on either side of his nose. "Took place over to Morgan City. If you know Morgan City, you know it's sort of a free-for-all zone. A good place to get lost and stay lost. Off-shore oil workers hang out there. Good pay for unskilled labor, and they need enough of it so they aren't too careful about social security cards and identification and such. Find almost anything over to Morgan City. And there's money around. Cash money. You don't pay those guys with no bank checks. They like to see the green foldin' money in the pay packets, so they can head straight over to the bar. No bankin' center, old Morgan City."

"Where is it?" Mary asked.

"Oh, 'bout ninety miles southwest. Our boy could've planned the robbery while he was livin' here, married to your cook as Jacques whatever. It was one of them million-dollar jobs, the once-in-a-lifetime kind of crime. You know, if we're gonna do it, let's do it right once, and not fool with robbin' the five-and-dime every other weekend."

He watched Mary closely as she reread part of the clipping, then passed it to Pierce. "You don't, uh, need glasses?" he asked softly.

"I'm wearing contact lenses."

Spraggue smiled. Mary rarely admitted it.

"I hate these things." Rawlins sighed. "Every time I have to put 'em on at work, I can just hear the young cops thinkin', poor old geezer, hope they put me out to pasture before I get that far gone. If I didn't need bifocals, I might get contacts, too. Not for vanity, you know—"

"I wear bifocal contact lenses," Mary said. "And not for vanity."

"They got those?"

"For pride. They take a little getting used to—"

"Hell with that. I'm gettin' some."

"Can we get back to business here?" Spraggue asked. "What about the other two robbers? Did the 'intensive police search' pan out?"

Rawlins didn't have to consult the notebook. "The only one they ever caught was the one they sent to Sisters of Mercy," he said with satisfaction. "The one in the article. Our 'James French.' And they had no luck tracin' any of his associates. Because there he was, in Morgan City, flat out lyin', givin' his name as James French, and here he was, in New Orleans, as Jacques somebody, and back home in the bayou, he was Joe Fontenot. I sort of remember the 'James French' they arrested pulled some kinda dumb-Cajun-po'-boy routine. You know, spoke only French or Cajun, and didn't seem sharp enough to really know what was goin' down."

"His picture must have been in the newspapers," Mary said.

"The only reason they caught French or Fontenot or whoever was 'cause he stopped a load of buckshot. He was in the hospital with bandages over most of his head. His leg was broken too and never rightly healed."

"Was he the one who killed the guard?" Mary asked.

"Nope. Matter of fact it was proved that he didn't. But we got here a statute called felony murder, the 'we're-all-in-this-together' law. If'n you commence to rob someone in cahoots with someone else and your buddy opens up with a shotgun and kills people, you're just as guilty as he is, even if you swear up and down you didn't even know he had a gun."

"But French was only in prison six years," Spraggue said. "Doesn't sound like very much for murder."

"Parole, I reckon." Rawlins regretfully replaced his glasses, riffled through his notebook. "He didn't get Murder One. He probably had a decent lawyer, and sometimes a judge ain't too enthusiastic about a felony murder rap. And I recollect that this guy was still chewed up pretty bad, gonna limp the rest of his life and all. Maybe the

102

judge thought he wouldn't return to a life of crime so quick with a limp.''

''He didn't,'' Mary said.

''What about the money?'' Spragigue asked.

Rawlins grinned. ''I was waitin' for that one. Turned out to be about five hundred thousand missing. They blew the million, left half the dough behind, and escaped with their skins, exceptin' for our boy, Fontenot. And here's an interestin' thing.'' The sergeant closed the notebook, removed his glasses, and gestured with them to emphasize his point. ''That money never turned up, and neither did anybody else who was in on the robbery with old James French.''

Twelve

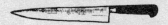

Spraggue lowered himself gingerly to the floor and adjusted his spine flat against the carpet. The bouncers' heave-ho throbbed in his lower back. He did ten repetitions of a relaxation exercise another former stage-fighting teacher had sworn by.

It didn't work.

Joseph Fontenot. Jacques Forte. And James French. Had there been other aliases, other identities? Spraggue felt the first twinge of sympathy, empathy really, for the dead man. He knew the desire to lead more than one short, preordained life, cut off from choice by circumstance of birth, making the kinds of decisions horses wearing blinders are allowed, beasts that see only the broad road ahead rather than the hundreds of fascinating, twisting alleys to each side. Acting let him live in other skins, experiment with other choices and other lives.

Private investigation held the same attraction. His greatest asset was his ability to blend in, with sure, quiet confidence, to play whatever role the situation required. He had that sort of face, unremarkable, flexible. If a play needed double casting, he was usually chosen.

Joe Fontenot, thief, con-man, bigamist, had lived more than one life. And in the real world, not on stage. Spragque wondered what it would be like—to change your name and your walk and your hair and your clothes, to begin again somewhere else, a new-minted stranger in a clean land, unshackled by the past.

How had 'James French' slipped his shackles? Even the best-behaved parolee was required to follow stringent rules. Paroled prisoners who might be able to lead authorities to half a million dollars and a murderer or two could expect closer supervision than most.

But 'French' had had a fine alias available—his own name—and a wife and daughter delighted to welcome him home, no questions asked.

Had Jeannine asked questions? Had Aimee known delight?

Sergeant Rawlins' revelations broke open the field of people who might have wanted Joe Fontenot dead. Cellmates, relatives of the murdered guard, partners in crime . . .

Fontenot would have sought his partners out, looking for rich reward for his silence. Not to mention his rightful share of the unrecovered half million.

Nineteen sixty-six was the year the robbery had taken place. 'Sixty-seven, the trial. Six years imprisonment. Nineteen seventy-three. Fontenot had been out of jail over ten years. But he'd started spreading money around only six months ago, when he'd gotten his legacy from his stepbrother, T-Bob. Or so Jeannine Fontenot said.

"Will there be anything else?" The high-gloss toes of Pierce's black shoes crushed the carpet a foot from Spragque's right shoulder. Spragque had been aware of the butler, polishing ashtrays, clinking glassware, wheeling the room-service cart into the hallway, but the sudden question startled him.

"Go to bed," Spraggue said. "Mary won't be back for hours yet."

"Good night, then."

"Turn off the light on your way out."

The darkness might help him concentrate, might ease him to sleep. When Aunt Mary returned from her pub-crawl with her detective sergeant squire, she would find him gently snoring on the carpet. Trip over him. *If* she came back. As she'd waved good-bye, Spraggue had caught a fleeting glimpse of the bohemian Mary Spraggue who lurked perilously near the surface of his aunt's staid Brahmin facade.

A horizontal bar of light gleamed like a neon rod in the darkness. Light spilled onto the carpet from under the closed door to an adjoining bedroom. Dora's room.

He listened to the pad of footsteps, the swish of cloth, as he got silently to his feet. How long the noises lasted he wasn't sure. A seam of light appeared at the side of the door, widened. A figure slipped into the room, glided over to the couch.

Spraggue flicked on the light switch.

He caught Dora bending over at the waist, patting at the couch. A brown handbag sat on one of the cushions. She grabbed it and turned to face him.

She expelled her breath slowly. "It is you," she said. There was nothing in her voice, neither relief nor apprehension.

"Going out?" She was wearing a neat beige suit, a pink blouse, tied at its high collar with a bow.

"No," she said. "Yes—maybe. I was just . . . I wanted to walk around outdoors." She wore lipstick. It was too bright for her pale face.

"It's late," Spraggue said. "Way past midnight."

"Midnight is late in Boston, not in New Orleans. I wanted, suddenly, to go somewhere with bright lights and music and people talking. Happy people. I wanted to see the old places. Maybe to sit on a bench at Preservation

Hall and watch the old men play joyful music. And Sweet Emma. I wondered if Sweet Emma still played the piano. She'd be an old woman now, or dead.''

"Preservation Hall closes early. Midnight, I think.'' Wouldn't Dora know that, Spragague wondered. She'd spent years here, not months.

"I forgot,'' she said quickly. "Maybe Pat O'Brien's then. Or—''

"I could go with you.''

"No, really, it was just an impulse. Better, probably, not to go. It used to be, in New Orleans, when I lived here, safe everywhere. Now they say there are muggings. Almost as bad as New York.''

"You're sure you don't want to go?''

She licked her lips and tried to make them smile. "No, *monsieur*.''

"I'm trying to help you, Dora. You know that, don't you?''

"Believe me, *monsieur*, this has nothing to do with that man's death. Because I am suspected unjustly of that, my whole life must be examined with a microscope?''

"If you want to go, go,'' Spragague said. Would the streets be crowded enough to let him follow her unnoticed?

She hesitated. "I'll stay.''

"Then sit down. And tell me more about your Jacques Forte.''

"I've told you what I can, what kind of man he was,'' Dora said helplessly. "It was long ago. I tried so hard to forget that it does not come back easily.''

She sat on the edge of the sofa, clutching her purse. If she hadn't left her handbag on the couch, she could have escaped the hotel easily. Her room had a door to the corridor. Had she been out before? Had Mary given her a key? Probably a duplicate at the desk anyway.

"What I need,'' Spragague said, "is a few facts. When and where and why and how.''

"I don't know what you mean,'' Dora said simply.

"What did you know about Jacques Forte when you married him?"

"I knew—I thought I knew—that I loved him."

Great. The naive reply of a seventeen-year-old.

"That's not what I—"

"I never met his family," Dora said defensively, "if that is what you mean."

"What did he tell you about his family? Why didn't you meet them?"

"There was some difficulty. His mother, he said, had died when he was young, and the woman his father had married after that, he was not close to. He did not like her, and his sisters were also estranged from him. I sympathized with him because I have no family myself."

"Friends, then," Sprague said. "Who were the witnesses at your wedding?"

"For me, Denise Michel stood up. It was not a grand wedding, you understand. A 'JP wedding,' he called it. A Justice of the Peace presides."

"Who was the best man?"

"No one, I think. His friend, I cannot remember the name, was called out of town, and the man at the office said it was not legally necessary."

"No friend to stand up at the ceremony?"

"The man was going to come and then could not at the last moment." Dora's voice flattened out and she finished lamely, "Or that is what Jacques told me."

"This friend, was he called T-Bob?"

"T-Bob," she repeated. "I think so. I remember that name. Petit Bob. He may have been the friend."

"You knew him?" Sprague said. "You met him?"

"No. Never. But I remember hearing his name."

Dead end. Roadblock.

"Where did you live?" Sprague asked. "You and Jacques?"

"In the Faubourg Marigny, a one-room apartment on Kerlerec Street."

108

"Did you look for the apartment together? Was his name on the lease?"

"No," Dora said quickly. "It was my apartment first where we were living. A nice apartment, not big enough for two perhaps, but we had so little money—"

"So this man with no friends or family moved into your apartment."

"Don't you think I've already told myself that I was a fool?" Dora's hands twisted the strap of her handbag. "I tell myself a sensible woman would choose a sauté pan, a paring knife, more carefully." She stared at the carpet, and her voice stayed low and flat with truthfulness that was as painful as an open wound. "I was no love-smitten school-girl. I was almost thirty years old—"

"Did your husband have a job, Dora? Did he go to work every morning?"

"He was a cook, *monsieur*, that I know. But he could not find work. He had been a saucier at one of the hotels, he said, but he was let go because of some contretemps with a foolish waiter. He looked every day for work. It was so hard for him, I think. A man must have work, for self-respect. I think sometimes he worked odd jobs, because he would come home very dirty, as if he did road-work, his hands calloused from digging. And then he would bring me flowers, sometimes beautiful flowers from the florist, sometimes a few faded flowers, sometimes blooms that looked like he'd picked them along the road. And he would have a little money for the rent. But he would be shame-faced. He would not tell me about this work."

"Luggage?" Spraggue said. "Photographs?"

"I never realized," Dora said in a faraway voice, "until after he was gone, how little of him was in the apartment. It was always my apartment. He brought but one suitcase full of clothing with him. That's all. I thought he was only poor. It's no disgrace to be poor, certainly."

"No disgrace," Spraggue agreed softly.

"He seemed a decent man," Dora said defiantly. "He was not some thief, some murderer!"

There was a deep stillness in the room.

"Why do you ask me these questions?"

"Because it might help solve his murder," Spraggue said finally.

"No," Dora said. "He was not killed by the past. He was killed with my *tanqueuer*—with my knife that people saw that afternoon. My knife case was unlocked only during the seminar. I locked it afterwards, and the key I wear around my neck. So it must have been someone from that seminar, from that dinner, from *today*."

There it was, Spraggue thought. She was right. No matter what newspaper clippings Rawlins pulled out of his pockets.

"Where were you going tonight?" he asked.

"Out, *monsieur*. Just out."

Thirteen

Buildings on either side of Aimee Fontenot's Esplanade Avenue apartment had a sheen of gentrification—new shutters, potted plants, Mardi Gras bunting. Aimee's place had weatherbeaten gray paint peeling off warped window frames. In the unlocked foyer, the name *Fontenot* was scratched on white adhesive tape stuck to a chipped wooden panel under a battered mailbox.

Spraggue rang her doorbell at nine the next morning. He figured nine o'clock would give her a chance to sleep off some of that bad champagne, but not enough time to recover from a hangover and get out of the house. He stabbed at the bell again. The muscles in his upper arms ached, and the memory of the bouncers made him hope the buzzer was exploding right in her eardrum.

No one answered. He wondered if she'd taken a paying customer to her bed. That might slow down her reactions. He hit the buzzer again, a staccato burst. Nothing.

Albert Flowers, skimming through the morning paper while waiting in the cab, was undismayed at Aimee's absence. He told Spraggue to cheer up, there was still one place where the woman might be, although Albert himself didn't understand why a girl would work at a place like that Bourbon Street dive and still hold a crummy clerk's job at the local K & B, where the Lord knew she couldn't make in two days what she'd earn on her back in an hour.

Aimee Fontenot looked as out of place behind the counter of the convenience store as a raven would have looked in a cage full of parakeets. Her handsome face glowered at the line of customers. Spraggue was sure that the words "Have a good day" never crossed her lips. She worked mechanically, just slowly enough to be slightly insulting, as if she knew she was too good for this job and this area and these people. She was rude without being blatantly disrespectful, insulting without giving specific cause for offense. It was a thorough performance and Spraggue caught the manager of the store glancing nervously at the woman from time to time as if wondering what he could do to get rid of the demon behind the cash register before she got rid of the queue of customers.

Spraggue picked up a packet of chewing gum at a garish display set deliberately low enough to tempt small children and got at the end of the line.

When it was his turn to pay, she recognized him. That he could tell from her eyes. "Forty-five cents," she said.

"I'll bet you have a fifteen-minute break coming up soon," Spraggue said. "Or we could meet later for lunch."

"That's a big forty-five minutes," she said, grabbing the dollar bill out of his hand. "And I like to spend it by myself."

"You don't look much like your mother."

"Yeah, but I'm hers. What I'm not sure is who my father was. But if I had a choice, I'd take just about anybody over old Joe, dead or alive."

The woman in line behind Spraggue coughed.

Spraggue pulled a roll of Life Savers off a display. "These, too," he said.

"Forty cents."

"Forty minutes. I'll buy you lunch."

"I brown-bag it."

"A drink."

"I don't drink."

"Not even champagne?"

The woman behind Spraggue tossed her purchase on the counter and made for the door with an annoyed grunt directed at the manager's ear.

"Problems, Aimee?" he said thunderously.

"No, Bobby," she said with a sneer that the man couldn't ignore.

"I'd rather you call me Mr. Thomas, Aimee."

"I'd rather you call me Miss Fontenot."

"Get out," the manager said in a tense whisper, trying to keep a jovial look on his face for the benefit of any curious customers. "You're fired. I knew this would happen. Dammit, I have had just about enough out of you—too damn good to do anything. Just get the hell out."

"Delighted," Aimee said cooly, as if she'd just accepted an invitation to tea. She ripped off the purple apron she wore over her black sweater, tossed it on the counter, and swung out the door before the startled manager had a chance to respond.

Spraggue followed. She was moving so quickly he had to sprint to catch up; he reached out to touch her shoulder and turn her around.

"Buy me breakfast," she said. "I haven't eaten yet and I left my damn lunch in his refrigerator and he's welcome to it."

She tucked her hand in the crook of his elbow and propelled him down the sidewalk.

"I'm sorry," he said.

"What for? Because I got fired? I would have gotten fired today or tomorrow or the next day. I get fired from jobs like that all the time."

"Why do you work there if you hate it so much?"

"To support my filthy habits. Eating. Paying rent."

"There are other jobs."

"Oh, you mean like last night? Yeah, I work the bar, but I need something steady, too. A little something so I can say no."

"There are other jobs besides bars and convenience stores."

"For Cajun girls who never finished high school? Don't like to say 'Yes, sir'? Don't type or file or take dictation? Man, it's fast food city out there, and that means taking orders for the rest of your life, or sucking up to some guy who wants to screw you so bad he'll marry you."

"Two," Sprague said to the smiling young woman who stood near the Please Wait To Be Seated sign in the dingy corner diner. He wondered if the hostess's glistening teeth hid a worldview as bleak as Aimee Fontenot's. They were ushered to a sparse wooden rectangle near a streaky window. Limp orange curtains partially blocked the sunlight.

"I'll find another job tomorrow," Aimee said. The anger seemed to melt out of her as soon as she sat down. It was replaced by a calculated sensuality, a deliberate tug at the tight black sweater.

"So fast?" he said.

"I never have trouble finding a job. Guys think I'm easy, they hire me."

Sprague found her anger more attractive than her sultry come-on. The anger was real.

"Of course," she said, with the first sign he'd seen of a grin twisting her mouth, "maybe the old man left me something in his will. Always supposing he left a will. He thought he'd live forever."

"I don't know if he left a will or not. Your mother would."

Aimee nodded thoughtfully. "She might even help me out, you know, now that the old guy's dead. Maybe I could scrape together enough to get out of here."

"And go where?"

"Someplace else," she said with a finality that signaled the end of that conversation.

She ordered bacon, eggs, and biscuits. Spraggue ordered coffee.

"What do you want?" she said, echoing the waitress after the waitress was gone. Her voice was breathier than the waitress's, her eyes narrowed. She made the question sound like a proposition.

"I want to know about your father."

"Why?" The anger was back.

"I want to find out who killed him."

"I don't want to know. Maybe it's a failure of the imagination," she said. "Maybe I just don't care."

"Did anybody else hate him worse than you did?"

"I doubt it."

"Why did you hate him?"

"Why should I tell you?"

"I want to know. I listen. I buy your breakfast. I'm cheaper than a shrink."

"You think I need therapy?"

"I think everybody needs therapy."

She laughed, but even her laugh had a bitterness to it, a rusty, unused quality.

"Here's my father for you." Her accent changed, got broader, so it sounded like a caricature of her mother's lilting Cajun speech. "He grow up po' an' ignorant. Dat good enough for him, dat good enough for me, all right, all right. I be a boy, maybe it be wort' send me to school. A boy, maybe make somet'ing outa himself. A girl only good for one t'ing." Her voice swung back to normal. "I mean it was bad enough when he didn't have a nickel to rub against a dime, but you saw that castle he was planning to open. Where did that money come from? And why didn't any of it come to me? That's an easy one. Because he never thought I was worth shit."

She washed a mouthful of bacon down with coffee, looked up at Spraggue, and said, "Aren't you going to tell

115

me that my daddy loved me and I misunderstood him? That's what shrinks say."

"Nope. He sounds like a bastard to me."

That twisted grin again. "Wish I was a bastard. Ever wish you were?"

"Nope."

"You're okay. You don't say much."

"Nope."

They stared at each other until she looked away.

"How old are you?" she asked, making the question intimate with her eyes.

"Older than you, kiddo."

"How old do you think I am?" She grabbed her weight of dark hair and lifted it to the top of her head, aping sophistication.

"Maybe eighteen, maybe not. I'm good at height and weight, not age."

"What do you really want out of me?" Bedroom eyes again. She seemed to be enjoying herself, sure of her effect on men.

"Where were you the night your father was killed?"

"Now let me see," she said, elaborately unconcerned. "What night was that? Wednesday? Thursday? It didn't make much of an impression on me. Probably at the bar. Maybe home. Maybe not."

"Helpful," Spraggue said dryly.

"Ask me for something else," she said, slipping further into her act, eyelashes lowered, voice husky.

"How about a key to your mother's house?"

It wasn't the right request. Her eyes snapped open. "To the restaurant? What the hell for?"

"I want to see what your dad kept around the house. Your mother's taking the position that Joe was a great man, and she won't hear a word against him. She's not going to let me look around."

"Especially after you lied to her," Aimee said smugly.

"Did you tell your mother I was a private investigator?"

116

"Called her right after you left last night."

Left. Spraggue thought that was an interesting way to describe his departure from the bar. "So now she'd never let me in."

"Why not break in? Ever hear of burglary?"

"Does that mean you won't give me the key?"

She took her time answering. "I'll think about it," she said. "I mean I hardly know you. I may want to tag along, just in case you find something valuable."

He didn't like it, but he thought that once he got the key he might be able to ditch her. "When will your mother be out of the house?"

"You work fast." She pushed her plate back with a satisfied sigh. "Let's see . . . Momma plays bridge tonight." She leaned her chin on her hand and looked up at him from under a fringe of silky lashes. "But not until tonight. . . . Whatever will we do until tonight?"

"I don't know," Spraggue said. Her eyes were incredibly dark.

"Make a few suggestions," she said. "It might make all the difference as to whether or not you get Momma's keys."

Fourteen

Spraggue stared into Aimee's eyes, drawn into them as if they were magnets. Her pupils were dilated. Not from drugs or darkness, he thought. Maybe she was slightly nearsighted. Maybe it was the enlarged pupils that made him picture a shade-darkened bedroom, quickened his breathing. It was an effect she knew how to use. "I'm old enough to—" he began.

"I wasn't going to suggest you adopt me." She reached under the table, rested her hand lightly on his thigh. "I had something else in mind entirely."

"Whatever it is," Spraggue said, keeping his voice level, "it'll have to wait a while." He folded four singles and stuck them under the corner of an ashtray to cover the check.

"Don't tell me you're not interested. I can tell when a guy's interested."

That wouldn't be too tough, Spraggue thought. Rule out any man obviously dead. "I'm interested," he admitted, keeping the depth of that interest carefully out of his voice. He was intrigued, both by her offer and by the reason behind it. At the Creole Strip, cash for service was a given. What kind of payment did she have in mind now? "But I have other things to do."

"Such as?"

"Make a phone call. Is there a phone around here?"

"On the corner. Can I come?"

"Okay. Seeing as how you have nothing to do for the afternoon."

She placed her hand back in the crook of his arm and matched his stride. Her fingers felt hot on his arm.

The hotel receptionist got the phone on one ring and cut him off before he finished giving Mary's name. But she punched the right extension and Mary answered crisply.

"How'd it go?" he said.

"Thank goodness." She breathed deeply and rushed on. "I won't have to leave that message after all, and I couldn't even figure out how to word it without everyone in the hotel realizing what was going on. Darling, I'll tell you all about everything at the police station—Where are you?"

"The police station?" Sprague repeated, not wanting to describe a phone booth that was getting progressively more crowded with Aimee Fontenot's deliberately taunting presence. "Is Rawlins back from Angola?"

"No, dear. Oh, I wish he were! His deputy called. Or I think it was his deputy, that man named Hayes. We have to get over there. That dreadful man, that fat recipe man, Harris Hampton, is making a terrific fuss, throwing some sort of fit really, and the police are out looking for you—"

"For me?"

"Darling, that's just it. He says you tried to kill him."

Fifteen

Aimee kept the come-hither in high gear until the moment she slid out of Flowers' cab, still refusing to part with the key to her mother's house. She insisted that it was "lost" and that maybe, if Spraggue came by tonight about eight, they might have a go at searching for it. Flowers' ears pricked up and a slow, easy grin settled over his face.

"Like I said," he murmured after she banged the door shut, "everybody oughta have a good time in New Orleans."

A shiny white van blocked the concrete walkway to the police station. Halfway up the path, a dark-haired woman adjusted her lapel mike and barked orders at two men carrying TV minicams emblazoned with the Channel 4 logo.

At Spraggue's hurried warning, Flowers sped by and turned the corner. They pulled up at the back entrance to the station.

"Better not wait," Spraggue said. "I'll call."

None of the cops at the station stepped forward and slapped the cuffs on him, but he could tell from their watchful eyes that he was no longer the fair-haired boy. He wished Rawlins were there.

A silent patrolman led him to a stuffy cubicle on the third floor. Aunt Mary, wearing a red knit dress, provided the only spot of color in the room. She was perched on a dreary beige sofa that was fractionally brighter than the stubble of carpet and the battered gray file cabinets. She used his entrance as an excuse to rise.

The man in the room towered over her. He was three shades darker than the coffee-colored Flowers, half again as tall, and had none of Flowers' easy diffidence.

"Sergeant Hayes," Mary said tartly, "I'd like you to meet my nephew, the notorious Michael Spraggue. Michael, Sergeant Hayes."

Hayes looked about thirty, except around his eyes, which stared out of a fiftyish snare of wrinkles. Spraggue split the difference and put him at forty. His handshake was firm and strong, with nothing to prove.

"Is there a problem, Sergeant?" Spraggue asked.

Hayes gave him the kind of glance you give a coin you've just flipped to see if it comes up heads or tails.

"A problem," Hayes repeated. "Yeah." He spoke in a slow deep bass, rich as cream.

The quarter had landed on its edge. Spraggue watched the sergeant's eyes, waiting for the coin to topple.

"We've got a citizen downstairs wants to swear out a complaint on you," Hayes rumbled. "Not for jaywalkin' either. The reason you're up here and not over in Interrogation with the cop who caught the squeal is 'cause somebody down there matched this up with the Fontenot homicide and swung it my way. Rawlins filled me in before he left for Angola. He told me about you, and he's a man whose judgment I generally trust. I've been stalling this guy. I thought maybe, if I got the two of you together, we might skip a lot of paperwork and publicity."

Publicity. Spraggue nodded slowly, remembering the TV cameras out front. The tall man's eyes never left his face.

121

"You want a lawyer?"

"Not if we can keep it informal," Sprague said.

The coin fell, heads or tails. Hayes made a decision. In whose favor, Sprague wasn't sure.

"I'll bring the complainant in," Hayes said. "He may insist on a lawyer. Or an armed guard." The sergeant's teeth flashed in what could have been either a grin or a grimace, and he walked out, leaving the door ajar.

Sprague folded himself onto the couch to wait. He was sure Aimee had a more comfortable sofa. . . .

Aunt Mary brought him back to reality with a whisper geared to foil any eavesdroppers at the open door. "I phoned Henri Fiorici in New York. As far as I'm concerned, he's out of it. No backbone. No motive."

"Didn't sound like he was desperately in love with Dora?"

"Once upon a time, maybe. But there's quite a leap between loving someone years ago and killing to protect that someone's honor two days ago."

"Agreed."

"More importantly"—Mary lowered her voice until she was almost inaudible—"Fontenot's financial position."

"You've got something good?"

"You have no idea how many banking regulations have been tossed in my face."

"Not as many as you know how to circumvent," Sprague said.

Mary smiled. "Well, Pierce and I phoned every local bank, inquiring, on behalf of the Foundation, into the financial status of Joseph Fontenot. It's a horribly common name in Louisiana, but fortunately, he had the middle initial *O*. For what, I can't imagine. I got a copy of one of his past paychecks from Paul Armand and worked from that. It turned up a very simple savings and checking account arrangement at the First National Bank of Commerce. None of Fontenot's dealings through First National in any way accounts for a sixty-thousand-dollar deposit on that restaurant. The man didn't have the money."

"Dead end," Spraggue said.

"You underestimate me, my dear. Once I had exhausted Joseph Fontenot, I began on Jacques Forte and James French. An accommodating head teller at the Hibernia Bank ferreted out Forte's account."

"He wouldn't have used James French again. French had a police record."

"If I'd thought of that it might have saved some time," Mary said. "But listen to this." She pulled a scrap of paper out of her gray leather handbag. "Jacques Forte opened one of those money market plus accounts on July tenth of last year with an initial deposit of twenty thousand dollars. Certified check. And he deposited ten thousand every month until he died."

Sergeant Hayes' voice boomed through the open door, requesting that Mr. Hampton follow him, please.

Spraggue stood up.

Hampton entered the room with the same practiced elegance that had carried him in and out of the Café Creole. He looked sleek and well-fed and pleased with himself. His thinning hair was lacquered in place. He patted the yellow handkerchief that stuck out of the pocket of his sky blue suit, and peered around the room. He seemed disappointed with its contents.

"Sit down." Hayes indicated the lumpy sofa with a commanding nod of his head.

Hampton obeyed with a hint of condescension, a monarch sitting in the presence of commoners.

Mary said, "I'll stand, if you don't mind."

Spraggue leaned against a cardboard-thin wall.

"Mr. Hampton," Hayes said. "You know these people?"

"I have spoken to Mrs. Spraggue-Hillman." His voice was silky soft. Spraggue had heard it on the radio. "She sat with Dora Levoyer at the banquet, at my table. I've seen Mr. Spraggue only on the stage, and in, I think, one movie. And, of course, last night.''

If Harris Hampton had seen him in one movie, he'd seen him in half the movies he'd made in his life, Spraggue thought. The man qualified as a fan. "You forgot to mention the Café Creole," Spraggue said. "Yesterday afternoon, when Paul Armand gave you the boot.''

The fat man turned to Sergeant Hayes. "Yes," he said cooly, "I'm almost sure, practically a hundred-percent sure, that this is the man. Same dark hair, same profile. By the way, has anyone asked for me? I was expecting someone to call. It's rather important.''

"They'll take a message at the desk," Hayes said shortly. "This is kind of important now. You're making a positive ID?''

"You mean, right now?" Hampton made a nervous noise, somewhere between a giggle and a snort. "Right here? I thought there'd be one-way glass. A lineup. Witness protection.''

"What's the point of a lineup?" Hayes said calmly. "Like you said, you already know Spraggue's face from the movies. It would have been a cinch to pull him out of a lineup.''

"And we met briefly yesterday afternoon," Spraggue reminded them, just for the pleasure of seeing Hampton squirm at the memory.

"So he's identified my nephew as my nephew," Mary said. "What next?''

"You can save your sarcasm, madam." Hampton's quiet dignity would have gone over big on a talk show. "I know what I saw.''

"I don't," Spraggue said.

"Go ahead and tell him," Sergeant Hayes suggested.

"I thought I could just swear out a complaint and leave.'' Hampton looked quickly from one face to the next. Realizing that he was the only one seated in the tiny room, he tried to reassert his dignity by standing.

124

"You could," the sergeant agreed. Every nuance of his deep voice, every line in his face, denied his words.

Hampton shot back his shirt cuff and stared at his wristwatch. "This is absolutely the last time I go through this today." He glared his defiance at Hayes, but met only a stony frown. "I was standing in front of my hotel last night, the Monteleone, when a car careened off the street and swerved right at me. If I hadn't jumped out of the way—"

"What kind of car?" Hayes asked.

"I told the other officer."

"Tell me."

"A dark-colored sedan. I don't drive. I don't know anything about cars."

"What time was it?"

"Oh, a little past three in the morning."

"Witnesses?"

"The doorman had gone inside the hotel. I was under the impression that the police would look for witnesses."

"What on earth were you doing 'standing outside' your hotel at three in the morning?" Aunt Mary asked.

"I may have to answer *your* questions," Hampton snapped at Hayes, "but I don't have to answer *hers*." He stared at his wristwatch again. "Could you check to see if someone's trying to get in touch with me?"

"I wonder what time this trash has to be taped by, to make the six o'clock news," Spraggue said.

Hampton's head jerked around.

Spraggue ignored him, spoke instead to Sergeant Hayes. "There's a TV camera crew camped out on your front lawn."

"A TV crew out front?" Hayes echoed in disgust. "If that's what this Mickey Mouse song and dance is all about—"

"Well, I don't know anything about it," Hampton said quickly. "Why should I? I mean, maybe someone spotted

125

me coming in. I am a celebrity, you know. Millions of people read my books, watch me on TV."

"Call the station," Spraggue said to Hayes. "Ten to one, they got an anonymous tip."

"If you've been wasting my time—" Hayes began.

"Wasting your time! I like that. I came in here to help you. You have a killer loose in the streets, waiting to kill again."

Hayes swallowed. "Some of our good citizens get pretty drunk in the Quarter around Mardi Gras time; they drive a little careless. Maybe that's what happened last night." The sergeant made his suggestion through clenched teeth.

"It was a deliberate attack. And I think it was this man. Unless he's got an alibi—"

"For three in the morning?" Spraggue shrugged his shoulders. He should have left that bar and gone home with Aimee Fontenot. He knew it.

"Did you call those TV people?" Hayes' arm started involuntarily for Hampton's collar. The food critic shrank back against the sofa.

"I have information!" Hampton said quickly. He offered his words to Hayes the way a beaten dog might offer a bone to his tormentor. "Important information, and every time I try to give it to one of your damned officers, they tell me to keep my mouth shut."

"About this so-called hit-and-run attempt?" Hayes asked.

"No." Hampton's pale eyes searched the room but failed to discover a sympathetic listener. "I admit, well, I may have made a mistake on that, like you said. It was dark."

"The story would get better coverage with my name in it," Spraggue said. "Right?"

"I have information concerning Joseph Fontenot's death." Hampton wasn't letting go of the spotlight now. "He was my friend, and I know who killed him. The police refuse to—"

126

"You want to make a statement or just read your speech to the TV cameras?" Hayes muttered.

"Nobody wants to hear the truth." Hampton ignored Hayes' interruption. "Just because Denise Michel is some kind of grande dame around here, some traditional, sacred cow, you're all pretending she had nothing to do with it. Denise Michel is a dangerous woman. She ought to be locked up. I told that other policeman and he's done absolutely nothing. Nothing!" Hampton carefully wiped his palms on his pantlegs, and sank back on the sofa. It creaked as it got the full benefit of his weight.

"I read the statement you gave Sergeant Rawlins," Hayes said. "As I recall, you didn't back up your suspicion with any facts."

"Hah! Denise Michel had a reason to kill Fontenot that a saint couldn't ignore. He was horning in on her cookbook deals. Cutting her out. I mean, why do you think she invited Dora down here in the first place? Undying friendship?" He tapped his massive chest, then lowered his voice to a confidential murmur. "No one knows the food and wine scene in New Orleans the way I do!"

Spraggue exchanged a long glance with Hayes, said, "Maybe the police haven't really taken advantage of your insider knowledge."

"Right." Hayes swallowed. "Maybe those other officers didn't realize who they were talking to."

Mary gave the sergeant an appreciative wink.

Hampton's round face settled into a satisfied smirk. "The police haven't got a clue," he said. "I mean, it's obvious, isn't it? Bigamy's still a crime, isn't it? Denise uses Dora to threaten Fontenot, says stay away from my publishing deals or you'll wind up with a lawsuit that'll cost you more than any royalties you'll ever earn. Not to mention your reputation and your marriage. Now, I'm not saying she set out to kill him. Maybe he tried to kill her and she fought back. She's one tough woman, Denise Michel. Butchers her own meat."

"And what would you say if I told you that she was in plain sight while the murder was committed? We have five, maybe seven witnesses who'll swear to it," Hayes said.

"Then she must have had a partner," Hampton insisted.

Little Paulette with the flowered dress, Spraggue thought. "How well did you know Joe Fontenot?" he asked.

"Oh, we moved in the same circles, you know."

"You called him a friend before. An old friend?"

"Depends on what you mean by that. I was one of the first people in New Orleans to pick up on the truly extraordinary things he was doing with Cajun food. I *made* his career, not that I ever expected any thanks for it. The power of the press, you know. And TV. There were a lot of chefs I could have talked about on the air, but Joseph was the most deserving. And the way people responded! Fontenot's cooking was absolutely the new wave. Anyone could see that! Even a fool like Denise Michel. I wouldn't be surprised if her next cookbook is a direct steal from Fontenot."

"Someone told me you were working on a cookbook yourself, Mr. Hampton," Mary said softly.

Hampton wiped his mouth with his yellow handkerchief, then made an effort at a boyish grin. "You know how people talk, my dear lady. I've dabbled in recipes before, but I really do feel that TV is my métier."

"This person," Mary went on, "intimated that not all your recipes belonged to you."

"It was Denise, wasn't it? Denise, Denise! Everyone worships that woman. It's hard to believe no one can see through her. Dora probably thinks of Denise as her friend."

"Shouldn't she?" asked Spraggue.

"Well, Denise always wanted to be more than Dora's friend, if you know what I mean," Hampton said with a sneer. "When Dora was abandoned, Denise practically took over her life. Oh, yes. She insisted that dear Dora move in with her, wanted to help dear Dora bring up the

128

baby. Quite a fine father Denise would have made, I always thought.''

"Wait a minute," Hayes said. "What baby? Slow down. What baby are you talking about?"

"Well, Dora thought she should give the baby up for adoption. Denise was all for keeping it. She thought a child would be better off without a man—" Something about the quality of the silence in the room made Hampton stop short. "It's nothing, really. Nothing to do with this business. It was a long time ago. I really didn't mean to mention it at all. I just get so upset about this insane hero-worship that seems to follow that Michel woman around."

"Keep talking," Hayes said. "I'll decide if it's important."

For a moment Hampton fought the impulse, but then the desire to gossip triumphed. "Well, the truth is Fontenot didn't just walk out on Dora," he said, trying to pretend he wasn't enjoying the sensation. "He dumped her when she got pregnant. Of course, the argument between Dora and Denise, that fizzled out. It was all academic anyway. The baby died."

"Whoa," Hayes said. "What are we talking about here? How did the baby die?"

Hampton shrugged. "All I know is she never brought it home from the hospital. Birth defects, I heard. Just a terrible story. I was certain Denise had told you. Or someone. Because you were so quick to hold Dora for Fontenot's murder. I mean, I'm sorry I had to be the one to blurt it out like that. Although," he turned eagerly to Aunt Mary, "it will make the case stronger for the defense, don't you think? If it does come to trial. I mean what kind of jury wouldn't understand? She could plea-bargain or something."

"Mr. Hampton," Hayes said, "we'll need an addition to your statement, concerning this baby."

"I don't know—"

"Or do you still want to press charges against Mr.

Spraggue? Because if you do, when you leave here, which might not be for quite some time, I can guarantee that I'll keep those annoying TV interviewers away from you. You'll leave by the back door, maybe under special guard, so that the newspapers don't try to bother you either."

"I don't want to press charges," Hampton muttered.

"You're free to go, Mr. Spraggue. Mrs. Hillman." Hayes nodded toward the door. He didn't want them around for any further revelations.

"One thing," Spraggue said quickly. "You knew Joseph Fontenot when he was married to Dora?"

"Oh, no. Not at all. I didn't know anything about the man apart from his cooking until, well, until everything came unstuck. As for Dora, I knew about some man she'd married. That's all. I mean he wasn't a great cook then, was he? Wasn't a name, just a hanger-on."

"That's enough," Hayes said. "You two are free to go."

The big man ushered them out and closed the door.

"I wonder," Mary said in the elevator on the way down to the ground floor, "where Hampton was in 1966."

"And what his name was," Spraggue said. "I wonder about that."

Sixteen

The lights on the second floor of Joe Fontenot's dream restaurant were out, except for a single lamp burning behind flimsy curtains in the front foyer, the kind of lamp one might leave on to scare away burglars. Spraggue strolled a block to a public phone and dialed Jeannine Fontenot's number. He was too far away to hear the ringing; it wouldn't carry across the heavy rain-soaked air. He imagined the bell in the upstairs apartment, echoing off empty walls. He let it ring fifteen times and hung up, satisfied.

It would have been easier if Aimee Fontenot had volunteered the key.

A rusty metal fire escape rising from the concrete slab of a back parking lot was the best bet. He didn't want to fool with the expensive alarm system Fontenot had installed to guard the first-floor restaurant. Funny how even cautious people ignored security from the second floor up. Good thing he'd noticed the cheap lock gracing the upstairs living room window and hurriedly flipped it open just before Jeannine Fontenot had demanded that the pseudo newsteam depart. No doubt Fontenot would have gotten around to changing it.

An occasional car hissed by on the rain-slicked road. The area, a mixture of residential and commercial property, was the sort of place where a solitary figure in a raincoat might be noticed by a passing patrol car. Sprague trusted to the camouflage of a grocery bag to blend into the scenery. A wonderful burglar's prop, he thought, the overstuffed innocuous brown grocery bag, binding the human race together with the shared tedium of universal checkout lines.

Through rain-spattered glass, the apartment over the restaurant seemed unreal, a cozy dreamlike scene glimpsed through a blurred TV screen. The window slipped up noiselessly. Mrs. Fontenot, bless her, hadn't checked the lock after his visit. But four inches open, the window caught.

Sprague felt no sense of unease, no breathlessness, no rush of adrenaline. He was immersed in his role, not a burglar, but an absent-minded, respectable homeowner. He had done this before, locked himself out. Such a bother, with all these groceries. And in the rain.

A little more exertion made the stubborn sash yield. Beads of sweat mingled with the rain on his neck.

He leaned inside the window and deposited the grocery bag on the floor. Then he stepped inside.

The living room couch was still dented where he'd sat chatting with Jeannine Fontenot. Newspapers lay in a pile near a sagging overstuffed chair. He wondered if Mrs. Fontenot had belatedly checked his byline.

He moved to the tiny vestibule, wiped his feet on the rubber doormat. His raincoat dripped on the beige rug. He checked the time. The hands of his wristwatch glowed in the dark. Nine o'clock. How late would the bridge game go?

He left the window open, calculating the time it would take him to escape once he heard the front door open downstairs. Would he hear it? The steps leading up to the apartment were wooden, bare. He tested a couple. They creaked satisfactorily. He'd hear them.

Where to begin? The feeble light from the lamp in the foyer didn't do much beyond casting mysterious shadows. The living room had few places of concealment. Cardboard boxes sat, fat and dusty, in a corner. Spragerue ruled them out. He'd given them a brief glance before and found only cookbooks and photo albums. Fontenot wouldn't have left the kind of documents he was looking for in packing boxes.

Were they kept in the house? Were they secret from Fontenot's wife? Did Jeannine know all about her husband's time in prison? Was the cooking trip to France a dream she had turned into reality through repetition and belief?

First assumption: Jeannine didn't know. He'd listened to her, watched her as she spoke about Joe's cooking odyssey to France, studied her hands, her eyes.

Would papers dealing with Fontenot's past be stowed in the restaurant safe? They'd need a safe in the restaurant, someplace to store the night's receipts before the morning's visit to the bank. But Jeannine would surely know the combination. Not the safe, then. Some secret place.

He paced the length of the hallway, identifying the rooms that opened on either side. Aside from the large front room and a tiny kitchen where shiny copper pans hung eerily overhead, there was a tiled yellow bathroom and a bedroom—very French Provincial, with a flowered bedspread and tight little rosebud curtains. He drew the shades down and clicked the button at the base of a bronze bedside lamp. The light gave off a rosy glow through a tinted shade. The bedroom held a chest of drawers made of dark carved mahogany, a dressing table with a triple mirror and a needlepoint bench, and two matching end tables. One was filled with a collection of old birthday cards and matchbooks, two bottles of pinkish nail enamel, a single knitting needle: Mrs. Fontenot's side of the bed. The other was cluttered with disordered bank statements—all from the legal First National account—cold remedies, a box of cough-drops, a lurid paperback novel. In the closet, behind clothes stuffed in too closely and laundered not often enough, was a shelf six feet off the ground. On tiptoe, Spraggue found dust and two hatboxes, each complete with flowered hat.

Jeannine hadn't begun the business of sorting through her husband's clothes, the sad giving-away and getting-rid-of process that follows any death. Spraggue went through Fontenot's clothes, searching every pocket. Two movie stubs, two nickels, and a dime.

The most promising room would be a study, someplace with a desk—a desk with a locked drawer or a secret cubbyhole. A room with a desk, that was what he was after.

And that was what he found. It opened off the bedroom, so small that it wouldn't have qualified as a closet in the old Spraggue mansion. It must have been windowless like a closet, so impenetrable was the dark.

He heard the noise and stopped dead, listening intently, his heartbeat thudding like a timpani.

"Come on in, snoop."

He reached in and rubbed the wall where the light switch should have been, found it, flicked it on. No need for secrecy anymore.

A woman tilted back in a leather armchair, legs bare to the thigh, elevated and crossed on the desk. Her hands were tucked behind her head, elbows spread wide. She wore a black cotton T-shirt, scoop-necked, sleeveless. Tight. A short black skirt. Her toes, poking out of black high-heeled sandals, were painted a garish green.

He couldn't see her face.

She wore a Mardi Gras mask, the visage of a great, feathered, sequined bird. Green, brown, purple. A cruel, predatory, hawklike bird.

She cawed that same rusty laugh she'd tried in the lunch-room. "So that's how you do it, huh?" Aimee Fontenot said. "You private snoopers."

134

He couldn't take his eyes off the mask. Her green toe-nails were like talons. "Been waiting long?"

Her eyes were outlined by green sequins. "Ever since Momma went out. I enjoyed myself. Burglary must be a real turn-on. I felt kind of like a burglar, all sneaky and excited."

"Not too boring for you?"

"Not at all." She lifted a strand of dark hair off the nape of her neck, twisted it around a finger, elaborately at ease.

"Take off the mask."

"Don't you like it? Doesn't it turn you on?"

"I like to see you when I talk to you."

"You're seeing me, aren't you?" She stretched, catlike, provocative. "I did some looking around while I waited."

"Find anything?"

"I found what you want, if that's what you're asking. But then I had a good idea where it might be."

"Are you planning to share your discovery?"

"It depends."

"On what?"

"Money."

"Money?"

"Yeah," she said. "You know I could call the cops and have you arrested."

"What for?"

"Breaking and entering."

"Who, me? A friend of yours? A man who bought you breakfast in a public place just hours ago?"

"Oh," she said, pointing a finger at him. It was maddening not to be able to read her face. "I get it. You'd tell them I invited you up—that we came in the front door together. And here we are all the way at the back of the house, practically in the bedroom. Why?" She mimicked innocence behind her ageless mask. "I'm sure I wouldn't know."

"The cops would probably figure it out," Spraggue said. "They're imaginative that way."

"Me and you? I thought you were old enough to be my father. And you're probably married."

"Nope."

"Divorced, then."

"Never been married."

"Well, the older they get the younger they like 'em," she said. The offer was plain, but the hostility behind the come-on warned him off.

"I'll look you up when I'm seventy," he said. "Right now, I'm after papers your father might have kept hidden— passports, identification—"

"The mask turn you off?" She tugged at something behind her head, shedding the bird mask.

"I like faces better."

"You like mine?" She uncrossed her legs, swiveled a few degrees, and posed, one leg still on the desk, one on the ground. "Think about what you'd be missing." The chair twisted back and forth, widening and narrowing the spread of her thighs. Her hand slipped into the desk drawer.

"I came here to get something."

"Quick in, quick out? Now that you've got the owner's daughter with you, it doesn't have to be like that. Unless that's the way you like it."

Sprague counted to ten. Her hand under the desktop worried him. The muscles in her forearm flexed.

"Come on," she said. "This is a deal, man. Normally I'm fifty bucks on a weeknight. But a quick screw in Daddy's bed would be a turn-on. I'll make it a freebie and hope old Joe's ghost is haunting the place."

He watched her hand, said, "I don't want to substitute for your daddy. I want his papers. That's all."

Her hand came out of the desk drawer slowly, talons long and green. She seemed to relax inside, as if the offer of sex had been obligatory business that had to be gotten out of the way before she could deal.

"I've got them," she said. "He kept all this stuff hidden up here, like his special recipes. He was scared to death of recipe thieves. People like that Harris Hampton wimp drove him crazy. He was always planning some sort of cookbook, and he said his recipes were valuable. What I'm interested in is how valuable.''

''I'm not after recipes.''

''You don't think I ought to ask for money, do you?''

''On the contrary, it warms my heart to see a daughter bargaining over her late father's secrets.''

''Look, I checked up on you. I knew I'd heard your name. You're rich. You were in this movie I saw. At least everybody says you were. I don't recognize you.''

''That's the nicest thing you've ever said to me.''

''Bullshit. You come from a filthy rich family and you're a goddamn movie star. People like you don't understand about money.''

''We know what it buys. And what it doesn't buy.''

''Oh, yeah,'' she said, and the sarcasm was heavy enough to turn the ''yeah'' into a three-syllable word. ''Tell me about it. Money can't buy you love.''

Spraggue kept his voice flat and low. ''Or a single second of your life to live over again.''

She tapped a green fingernail against the manila folder she had slid out from under the desk blotter. ''It's gonna buy whatever's in here. Sight unseen. Unless you'd rather watch it burn.''

''I take it you've looked through the folder.''

''Skimmed through.''

''No curiosity? I might be able to explain some of the obscure parts to you.''

''I'm curious—to see how much you'll offer.''

''Let's start the bidding at the top then. I offer one book of matches.''

''Huh?''

''You'd sell me yesterday's newspaper for a dollar, wouldn't you?''

''With pleasure,'' she said, her face as implacable as the bird mask. ''People like you deserve to be taken.''

"Yeah, we're so much more reprehensible than the honest poor who'd sell their father out for a few bucks."

Her hand went for the drawer. He swept the papers off the desk with one hand and caught her arm with the other. The desk chair spun her helplessly for an instant, then she jammed her feet against the ground and fought back. He pinioned her right arm behind her, and jerked up until she cried out.

The folder fell to the floor. All the sheets of paper inside fanned out across the carpet.

Blanks.

"There *were* papers," she said faintly. "There *were*—I came to get them, but they were already gone. Momma must have gotten rid of them."

"Would you have sold them if you had found them?"

"You bet."

"No matter what they said?"

"Joe didn't waste any time trying to protect me. I don't owe him."

No point in shoving her elbow higher. No point at all. Somebody had already hurt her more than he ever could.

"I'm going to let you go," he said. "You can holler police; you can do whatever you damn well want, but I'm going to search this room."

"Okay," she said. "Fine by me."

She didn't rub her arm when he loosened his grip. One corner of her mouth shifted in a faint grimace, but that was all the outward show she allowed her pain. "There's nothing here. Anything he'd kept secret would have been in this file at the back of the locked drawer. He kept his recipes there, like I said, and that was as sacred as anything got with him, a recipe. I've been through it, and that's all there is."

"And of course, I believe you, but I'm going to look anyway."

"Of course."

There was one item that Aimee hadn't noticed. It wasn't

a recipe, but a cutting from a newspaper, folded and scrunched up at the bottom of the drawer.

"What's that?" she asked quickly.

Spraggue pocketed it. "You want it, you get it," he said.

Aimee folded her arms across her chest. The green talons made half-moon dents in the bare flesh of her upper arms.

In the top desk drawer was a penknife. Its open blade was not quite three inches of rusty steel. Just long enough to make him glad he hadn't taken Aimee Fontenot up on her offer.

Just long enough to make him wonder where she really was the night her father died.

Seventeen

The message at the Imperial Orleans' front desk said simply: *Napoleon House.*

Spraggue changed his sweat-soaked T-shirt for a short-sleeved sport shirt, and made sure the newspaper clipping was still in his pants pocket. He left his trench coat tossed over a chair.

It was hardly a walk, just to the corner of Conti and Chartres, pronounced "CONT-eye" and "CHAR-ters" to trip up the tourists. The rain had ceased; a faint Mississippi River breeze brushed against his bare arms. It felt clean after Joe Fontenot's stuffy den, Joe Fontenot's angry daughter.

Napoleon House was a bar he had frequented during that apprentice-actor summer. The peeled-paint walls, the orange glow from the hanging lamps, the spinning Casablanca fans were the same, like a set from an old film that had been carefully preserved. In spite of the heat, he shivered. He felt like he was walking into a scene from his past, from some other life he'd once lived, and he wondered if actors from that old company would rise and spout lines from *Cat on a Hot Tin Roof*, then invite him to join them at the round wooden table. Would they recognize him, see Spraggue, the earnest young actor-to-be, in Spraggue, the middle-aged snoop? Or had he altered completely, in both appearance and attitude? If he took a new name, the way Fontenot had, would anyone know him?

Strains of Vivaldi drifted through the room and the music seemed to come out of the past as well. The arched mirrored bar still held an ivory bust of Napoleon. Pictures of the Little Emperor covered one wall, highlighted all the others. Some long dead mayor of New Orleans had offered the house to Napoleon, a refuge for the exile. But Napoleon had died on St. Helena before his escape could be engineered, and only the memorabilia made it to the bar.

He couldn't see Aunt Mary. He crossed the room and peered into an alcove by the telephone. Two gray-haired men studied a chess board. He tried the niche next door, and interrupted young love. The two heads bent over the table, one dark, one blonde, didn't even acknowledge his presence, so hypnotized was each by the other. A private room opened off the far wall, next to the dark wooden sideboard. Mary wasn't alone.

"Hi," Spraggue said. "When did you get back?"

Sergeant Rawlins turned, grinned his easy, deceptive grin. "Just a while ago."

Spraggue had a feeling that they hadn't been discussing the case. "Sorry to interrupt," he said, raising one eyebrow.

"If I hadn't wanted you to join us," Mary said dryly, "I would hardly have left you a message." She drew a waiter to her without lifting a finger, using the mysterious power she exerted over restaurant personnel. "Another glass, please," she said. "You'll have brandy?"

"I'm sure Napoleon would approve."

"Rawl has been telling me about his trip to Angola," she said.

Maybe, Spraggue mused, but they'd gone on to other things.

Like a mind reader, Rawlins answered the unspoken thought. "Didn't take too long 'cause I didn't learn a whole lot."

"Nonsense," Mary said. "You did a marvelous job. Can I tell him the best part?" Spraggue couldn't see her right hand—or Rawlins' left. He hoped they were holding hands under the table.

"Sure." Rawl grinned. "Then I'll know what the best part is."

"Joseph Fontenot did not acquire his chef's training in France. He—No." She caught herself, and smiled brilliantly up at the sergeant. "You tell it, Rawl. You got it from the horse's mouth."

"Well, the horse's mouth would be the warden, old Jason Beaumont," Rawl said. "But come to think of it, he's often mistaken for some other portion of a horse's anatomy." He was enjoying himself and his drawl got lazier and more pronounced. "Same warden as was up there when James French was inside."

"And," Mary said, "he remembered French right off."

"He sure did." One corner of Rawl's mouth turned up. "It's funny, I thought he'd have to look it up or somethin'. But no, his eyes bugged out and he got kind of excited. I only realized a little later that he was droolin' over the thought that I might have brought this here French fellow back with me for another dose of prison."

"Huh?" Spraggue made the noise to get Rawlins' attention away from Mary.

"You know what task they assigned poor James French when he was in jail?" Rawlins continued. "He was the cook. And old Beaumont says he never had it so good as when French was head cook, and if he'd known how bad the cooks were gonna get after him, he never would have okayed time off for good behavior. He would have framed him for something, and kept him in jail forever. I mean,

142

it's been twelve years, and the warden's mouth still waters at the thought of the meals he had when French was doing the cooking.''

"Jailed for natural life on grounds of gourmet cooking," Mary chimed in. "No appeals."

"Warden said they about had a riot when the rest of the jailbirds realized French was gone. They'd gotten into taking him for granted."

"Did the warden talk about anything besides food?" Spraggue asked.

Rawlins sighed. "He said that French kept to himself. That he played poor dumb Cajun for all it was worth. That he cooked, period. That he didn't have a close friend. That he didn't write letters or get letters. That he didn't get money from the outside. That he was stubborn and uncooperative, and the damnedest fine cook."

Mary set her glass down on the table with a bang. "Listen. If the rumor got around that Joe Fontenot was a graduate of Angola State instead of Cordon Bleu, it could have been more than embarrassing for him, especially with a new restaurant opening up and a cookbook deal on the horizon. Maybe he was being blackmailed."

Rawlins considered it, sipped brandy. "If he were bein' blackmailed, why would the blackmailer kill a goose busy doin' the golden-egg bit?"

"Self-defense?" Mary suggested. "Maybe Fontenot was trying to kill the blackmailer."

"No signs of a struggle at the scene," Rawlins said. "Lab's got no evidence that Fontenot marked his killer. No scrapin's of skin under his fingernails or anything like that."

"And," Spraggue added, "Fontenot was making large cash deposits at the bank, not withdrawing money to pay blackmail."

"Was he, now?" Rawlins murmured.

"Damn," Mary said, "I forgot about that."

143

"Did you get anything else at Angola?" Spraggue asked Rawlins.

"I checked more prison files than you'd believe. I got names and addresses of guys who did time with French. Some of 'em are back in prison, some on parole, some have gone arrow-straight. But, according to the warden, none of them were James French's particular pals."

Mary poured brandy into Rawlins' glass. He smiled at her, took a drink, and went on.

"The warden says French never spoke a word about that holdup, and never said squat about the money or who his pals were. They tried to make a deal with him. If he'd split on his buddies, he might have gotten away scot-free. He wasn't the one who'd fired the shot. If they'd gotten the money and the killer, they might have released him on time already served. The warden put that to French in person, and French just looked at him and never said word one."

"Which gives us a lot to go on," Mary said gloomily.

"Well," Rawlins said, "there was one odd incident . . ."

"Rawl, have you been holding out on me?" Mary's look didn't match the severity of her voice.

"Just saving the best for last. Evidently, a son of the armored-car guard, the man who was killed in the robbery, tried to visit James French in prison."

"Why?"

"Said he wanted to assure his daddy's killer that he forgave him, that he wasn't interested in revenge, that vengeance belongeth to the Lord. Also wanted to convert French, believed that if he could convert the killer of his father, his own flock would regard him with greater respect." Rawl was reading bits and pieces of this from notes he'd scrawled on the backs of business cards.

"His own flock?"

"He's a sort of a preacher. Name of Archibald Renner. They had a bit of a problem with him. He hung around one day until French was out in the exercise yard, then started an open-air revival meeting, which the rest of the prisoners didn't find too amusin'. They all hooted him down, which brought about a general revocation of privileges for the population.''

Mary lifted the brandy snifter to her mouth. "I wonder if the preacher ever found out who French really was. And if he was as forgiving as all that.''

"I've got an address for him. And it's local.''

"Now that's wonderful,'' Mary said. "Very promising.''

Rawlins sighed deeply, shook his head. The dim overhead lights gave his white hair a reddish cast. "It's farfetched and unlikely,'' he said gently, staring at Spraggue to avoid looking at Mary. "I hate to say it, believe me, but let's face facts. Sergeant Hayes left a report on my desk. He checked out Harris Hampton's statement.''

Mary knew he was really talking to her, and she answered. "Harris Hampton said, among other things, that my nephew tried to kill him. So I don't intend to believe any part of his nonsense.''

"Your privilege, Mrs. Hillman.'' The atmosphere chilled. Spraggue knew they were long since past the formal address stage. "But all the same, Hayes did check, and a stillborn child was born to a Dora Forte in St. Savior's Hospital about the same time James French was beginning his tour as cook of the state prison at Angola, which means he not only left her, but he left her pregnant. She may have blamed the baby's death on him. A long time ago, yes, but some things time doesn't heal, in spite of what folks say.''

"Oh, Dora,'' Mary said, under her breath.

Rawl said, "I want you to realize how bad that's gonna sound in court.''

"Other people could have killed Fontenot!'' Mary said angrily. "Denise Michel. She hated the man. He tried to steal her cookbook contracts, and her alibi's no good if that waitress, Pauline, Paulette, whatever! was her partner. Harris Hampton stole recipes from Fontenot, and Fontenot

145

vowed revenge. Fontenot quit working for Paul Armand. There may have been something behind that. Jeannine Fontenot benefitted from her husband's death. She'll open that restaurant now—''

"Could have," Rawlins said. "Might have."

"But you can't stop now," Mary insisted. "You'll see this preacher, this Archibald Renner?"

Rawlins studied the grain of the wooden table. "I have other cases. The taxpayers like it when I work on all of them, impartially. Your nephew can deal with Renner."

"Or I can," Mary said.

"Better leave it to—" Rawl began.

"Whoa. I have a clue of my own to follow." Spraggue quickly displayed his folded newspaper clipping, hoping to forestall the blow-up that would inevitably follow if Rawlins suggested there was anything on God's earth that Mary should leave to someone else. "It's from the *Times-Picayune*. I won't say where I got it, but it was someplace where Joe Fontenot used to keep important papers. And, by the way, all those papers have mysteriously disappeared, according to Fontenot's undevoted and unreliable daughter. This got left behind. Go ahead, read it."

MYSTERY SKELETON IN ST. LOUIS CEMETERY was the headline.

"Hmmph," Mary said. "Mystery skeleton indeed. That's all we need."

"Read," Spraggue said sternly. He knew the four brief paragraphs by heart.

MYSTERY SKELETON IN ST. LOUIS CEMETERY

The funeral of a member of one of Louisiana's oldest families was marred yesterday by a gruesome discovery.

Thomas Despardieu, 78, of Jefferson Parish, last surviving son of Emile and Angela Despardieu, for whom Despardieu Square is named, was to be laid to rest in the family plot in St. Louis Cemetery, Number Three, yesterday. Burial was delayed and police were called to the location by the head of the cemetery workers when, in preparation for the event, workers opened the tomb.

According to archdiocesan records, the last burial in this vault of the Despardieu tomb, one of the most beautiful of the marble tombs in the cemetery, took place nineteen years ago, the year Despardieu's sister died. Expecting a single skeleton in the vault, the cemetery workers were taken aback to find two skeletons where only one should have been.

The Medical Examiner for the parish was immediately called and examinations will be carried out on the unidentified body.

Rawlins pulled the clip closer, frowning over it. "I remember this," he said. "Two days' wonder, then no more information."

"You found this at Fontenot's home?" Mary asked.

"Skip the location and concentrate on the clipping. Two things intrigue me," Spraggue said.

"What?" Rawlins said. "You break into the house?"

Spraggue ignored the second question. "Number one," he said. "The word 'nineteen' has been circled. The tomb was last opened for a funeral nineteen years ago. Number two, the date on the corner of the clipping is July second. Of last year."

"Doesn't ring bells," Mary said.

"On July tenth, Fontenot made a twenty-thousand-dollar deposit in a bank account. On July fifteenth, he made a sixty-thousand-dollar down payment on a new restaurant."

Eighteen

In his dream, Aimee Fontenot laughed contemptuously, her hidden lips mocking him behind that gaudy feather mask. She wore the mask and nothing else. Her imagined nakedness was bold, matter-of-fact, yet not unarousing. She was too shy to remove her mask, so her face became the truly erotic part of her. But when she took the mask off, her face had changed, and it was Dora under the mask. The body grew older, the breasts drooped. The miraculous logic of the dream clothed the altered, stretched body in chef's white and turned it into a grim-faced Denise Michel. She was grasping something behind her back with a pressure that made the muscles in her forearm bulge, and Spraggue knew it was a butcher knife, crying for blood. Paul Armand and Henri Fiorici held Harris Hampton down on a wooden table, and Spraggue was relieved that Hampton was the chosen victim. Everything would be all right now because Fontenot would be alive again once Hampton had been sacrificed on the kitchen altar. It made sense. But the figure was masked again, not with the evil bird mask Aimee had worn, but with another one he had seen in a shop window, the massive face of some implacable wolf-God, yellow and purple, with staring holes for eyes. He tried to see the eyes beyond the holes, but the sockets were empty. The now sexless figure was robed in black, like some obscene priest. The knife whipped out from behind its back, the extension of cruel claws. Voices were wailing, screaming, crying—

The voices, at least, were real. Spraggue woke up sweating, clutching the pastel blue Imperial Orleans' comforter like a shield. The clock said eight-thirty, and the fuzz on his tongue said he'd drunk too much brandy the night before.

"No! You are absolutely wrong! Mistaken—"

The voice was Dora's, and because the words were the loudest he'd ever heard her speak, Spraggue yanked on a pair of jeans and defied the inner voice that told him getting up was not wise in his present state.

He was still sweating when he walked into the suite's living room. The air-conditioning had no effect on the kind of perspiration that came from spinning nightmares.

Dora, wearing a shapeless white terry robe, sat crumpled on the sofa, bent so far forward her head almost touched her knees. Her wispy hair and cupped hands hid her face. Her shoulders jerked and shuddered, but her crying was soundless.

Aunt Mary was pacing, staring at her shoes as they traced a pattern in the gold carpet. She wore the same pale pink suit she'd worn last night, slightly rumpled and creased. No chance to change if she hadn't slept at the hotel. Spraggue's eyebrows arched in a quiet salute to Gorman Rawlins. One glance at Mary's stern face told him a flippant remark was hardly in order.

Pierce was ineffectually patting Dora on the back, looking as uncomfortable as Spraggue had ever seen him.

Mary lifted her head when he came in. "I'm sorry if we woke you," she said automatically. "My fault. I thought

149

I ought to tell her. What they'll say at the trial—about the child—what that awful Hampton man said."

Spraggue winced. Mary charged where angels feared to tread.

"All I really made out was 'No!,' " Spraggue said. "If she denies it, and they have the hospital records, it'll look bad."

Pierce said firmly, "I think the word is 'repressed.' I hardly think she can be blamed for repressing such an obviously unacceptable event as—"

"No!" Dora said too loudly. "You're wrong."

"Wrong about what, Dora?" Spraggue said it gently, dropping it into a vacuum.

"My baby's not dead."

Pierce patted her clumsily. Mary said softly, "I'll call the hotel doctor. He can refer us to—"

"What do you mean?" Spraggue asked Dora, ignoring his aunt, who froze with one hand on the ornate phone.

"I hardly think we should cross-examine her now," Mary said. "I'm sorry I brought the whole business up. I had no idea—"

"Maybe Dora's not suffering from delusions, Aunt Mary," Spraggue said. "Maybe she's doing her best to answer your question. You know where you are, don't you, Dora?"

"Of course. Why are you asking me that? I'm in a hotel room. I'm accused of killing a man, and now you say my baby died."

"That's what the hospital records show."

"No. They don't. I gave the baby up for adoption. I couldn't take care of the baby by myself. Denise said I could, but I couldn't. I did what was best for the baby. They told me, they promised me . . ."

"Who promised you?"

"The doctor, the nurse—I remember her name, Elise. The nurse was my friend. Once I thought I would name the baby for her if it was a girl. Elise—such a pretty name.

150

She said it would be best, adoption. Find the baby a good home."

"Oh, Dora," Mary said. "I'm sorry."

"I can't do this anymore," Dora said. Her voice was soft now, clear but bewildered. "I can't talk about this. I've talked about it to myself for twenty years, trying to decide if I did—did the right thing. I can't change what I did then. I can't be what I was before. There's no point to all this talking."

She got up very carefully, as if she didn't trust her bones to carry her weight. Her words were clipped and dry. Brittle. She walked to the door of her room, taking steps as tentatively as a toddler afraid to fall, small baby steps, falteringly slow. The door closed and the bolt twisted home.

"Well," Mary said into a long silence, "I am heartily sorry I started that."

Spraggue blew out his breath and slumped on the sofa. "I probably would have done the same thing. She shouldn't have to face the fact that they know about the baby on the witness stand."

"And it may come to that?"

"Rawl's right. The grand jury will have plenty of reason to indict. It *was* her knife. All this other stuff is pie-in-the-sky. What if? Maybe? Fontenot may have lived a shady secret life, but hasn't Dora? Hasn't everybody?"

"All right." Mary closed the issue with a sigh. "I'm going to shower and change. And then I'm going out to find this Archibald Renner. Don't worry, I'll take Pierce with me. Perhaps on rereading the scriptures Brother Archibald found he disagreed with the 'Vengeance is mine, sayeth the Lord' part. Or maybe he sees himself as the Lord's deputy."

"He would still have had to get into the Imperial Orleans," Spraggue said.

"Well, the Lord works in mysterious ways."

Nineteen

The news media knew little more about the surplus skeleton than the initial article had disclosed. Spraggue, seated on a hard plank bench in a basement room of the Times-Picayune Building, read every word of the follow-up stories, and found one fact amid much speculation: the bones had been turned over to the coroner of Orleans Parish.

The Coroner's Office occupied one wing of the big Criminal Court Building on Tulane Avenue. There, Spraggue ran full tilt into bureaucracy at its finest. The coroner was busy. What did it concern? Had he come to identify the remains? Was he with a newspaper? Ah, the police. And where was his identification? Certainly, they would call Detective Rawlins. Always glad to cooperate with the police. Oh dear, Detective Rawlins was not in, and not to be reached. Alas. So sorry, but there was no way the busy coroner could be disturbed for someone who might turn out to be no one. It was the relentless, phony politeness that got to him in the end. The smiles. The final

"Have a nice day" that made him want to chip someone's shiny front teeth.

Albert Flowers had parked his cab out front, blocking a fireplug. Sprague handed him the clipping and waited while he read. "This cemetery," Sprague said, "St. Louis, Number Three. You know where that is?"

" 'Course I do. Wanna lift?"

"Yeah."

"You lookin' pale this morning, but you look lively for a cemetery," Flowers said.

"Drive the cab," Sprague said.

The entrance to St. Louis, Number Three, the newest of the old St. Louis cemeteries, was marked by heavy wrought-iron gates, arched and spiky. The dying afternoon light and the faint pattering rain gave the white tombs a pearly shine. They looked like crammed-together mansions in some grandiose city replicated in miniature.

"Cities of the Dead," Flowers said softly.

"Huh?" Sprague was surprised to find his thought spoken aloud.

"They look like your northern cemeteries?"

"Spookier," Sprague said.

"Because the water table is so high, we can't bury under the ground," Flowers said. "The grave fills with water as soon as you're six inches down. The oldest tombs, like in this place and the other two St. Louis cemeteries, were made of brick and whitewashed. Then the rich folk got it into their heads that it would be fine to rest in fancy marble tombs for all eternity. For a while they had a real contest going. Imported marble and sculptors. And not just the rich families bought into it. The societies got involved, the benevolent societies and the Italian-American Society, and everybody had to have the best architect and the finest building materials. New Orleans is funny about burials. Down here, All Saints' Day is a big holiday, and everybody goes to the graveyards with flowers."

They stopped the car at the end of a narrow lane. The

153

cemetery seemed deserted, a separate country cut off from the living city by high brick and stone walls. The walls were patchworked with carved tablets and dotted with tiny vases of pallid, wilted flowers.

"Are there tombs in the walls?" Spraggue asked.

"Yep. The old Creole families used to call those the 'fours,' the ovens. If your family ain't so high-tone to warrant a big tomb, you can rent or buy one or two of the ovens. Some are rented for a year, ten years, some forever."

"Rented?" Spraggue repeated, puzzled.

"Yeah. You see how these have sunk right into the ground here?"

Near one corner of the cemetery, the bottom of the wall had disappeared into the mud, taking with it the words carved on a crumbling marker. LYDIA, ÉPOUSE DE HU—was all that was left above ground. Most of the inscriptions were in French.

"What do you mean, 'rent' a tomb? 'Rent' means you can get evicted."

"Right," Flowers said. "They use a single vault for a lot of burials here. I guess that's one reason why family's so important in New Orleans. You really are going to spend eternity in the company of your folks. See, these family tombs, even the real rich tombs, they got two, three ovens, two, three vaults, in 'em, that's all. So let's say old Granny Money dies and she's the first Money to go, and they build this grand tomb for her. And they have a nice coffin, and they chuck it in the oven, and they seal it up with a marble plaque, and oops, 'fore you know it, Granpa Money is gone, too. Big funeral. They put him in the bottom oven. Now you might say the tomb is full, but the very next year, Uncle Alfred Money kicks the bucket. Now are these rich people gonna commission another architect and haul another load of Italian marble over here when they've already got a perfectly good family tomb? No way. So what they do is, if a year and a day's passed since Granny's funeral, they open up her oven, and they burn the casket and stuff. And they sweep old Granny's bones to the back of the tomb, into what the Creoles call the *caveau*—sort of a pit down below—and Uncle Alfred gets her spot, for at least a year and a day, until the next family funeral comes along.''

"You're better than a tour guide," Spraggue said.

"It's one of them tourist things, like the hoodoo charms. Folks always ask about the graveyards," Flowers said. "And workin' the airport like I do, I consider myself a guide as well as a taxi service.''

"What happens if there's a disaster?" Spraggue asked. "A fire? Say three members of the family are killed at once. Or what if Uncle Alfred hadn't waited a year and a day?''

"Well, they rent one of the wall ovens then, until space is available in the family tomb. And sometimes space never gets available. Say you got a real black sheep in the family. Lots of them never end up in the family vault at all. If you have a fight with the family in New Orleans, you don't just get disinherited. You get tossed out of your eternal restin' place. And the tradition here is for the man to join his wife's family, in the tombs at least. So you got to get on with the folks, or your body's just gonna get chucked in one of the wall ovens, and you'll never mingle your bones with your mother-in-law's. It's real tricky 'round here, gettin' buried.''

They set off down one of the avenues of tombs. Spraggue read the names on the markers. French names. LaForge, and Fabre, and Darriere. La Famille Lafontaine. Danielle Lafontaine, 1882–1884. Two years of life distilled to a single line of carved print. Was Dora's nameless child alive? Or buried in such marble splendor?

The caretaker lived in a whitewashed shack smaller than some of the tombs. He was just finishing up lunch. A paper cup, dark with coffee, sat on a tiny desk near a dusty phone. The whiskey smell said the color was more camouflage than coffee. The man was dressed in coveralls that had started out white some years ago. He wore a billed cap pulled down over his eyes, was a shade or two lighter than his suspicious coffee, and had a wary cast to his eye as he looked up at his two unexpected guests.

"Yeah? So me, what can I do for you, eh?" he said, and Spraggue was reminded of a French-Canadian he'd known who'd lived for years in Maine and developed his own blend of Yankee French. This man's voice was softer. He blurred the edges of his words, sliding one into the other.

Spraggue displayed the *Times-Picayune* article. The man recognized it, and a smile spread over his face.

"More o' them news guys?" the man in coveralls said with satisfaction. "Long time gone by. Half year, maybe. Ain't it a dead issue yet?" He laughed, and Spraggue bet he had three hundred more dead jokes where that one came from. He steeled himself.

"You the one found the corpse?" Flowers asked quickly, as if he, too, wanted to ward off an avalanche of graveyard humor.

"Couldn't right call it a corpse, after all this time," the caretaker said. "Say it a skeleton. But me, I be there sure enough. I be there."

"I'm interested in hearing exactly what happened that day," Spraggue said. "Very interested, Mr. . . ."

"Mr. Breaux. Jack Breaux."

Spraggue folded a ten-dollar bill into the caretaker's hand.

"You not a cop," the man said.

"It doesn't matter who I am."

"I don't want get in no trouble."

"How can you get in trouble talking about the dead?" Spraggue asked.

"You right 'bout that, okay. They don't care how much you gossip 'bout them, these guys."

"Tell me about the day the extra body was found."

156

"Want some coffee?"

"Thanks."

Paper cups were filled with hot brown liquid from a pan that had been sitting on a portable electric ring. A paper sack containing a pint bottle of Southern Comfort was offered and refused.

It was too crowded for the three of them in the tiny office. They went outside in the mist, and sat on a bench in front of one of the tombs.

Breaux slurped his adulterated coffee, said, "Now let me go back to that day. Wasn't a good one, that I recall. Rainy an' gloomy, like this. Nothin' unusual 'bout the weather, an' not much unusual 'bout the day. We don' do a lot of funerals here no more. This cemetery mostly all filled up, an' so old we don' get much business no more. Few of the old families still use their tombs, all right, an' people come visit. Busy sometimes, but more wit' upkeep than wit' newcomers. Now that day we got a funeral fo' the Despardieu tomb, which is a real pretty one, on yo' left as you come in the gate—"

"Could we see it?" Spraggue asked.

"I'm s'posed to stay by the shack, okay, case the phone ring or somethin'."

"But you have to leave it sometimes," Flowers said. "Come on. This story needs pictures to go along with it."

"Okay, *cher*," Jack Breaux said. "Follow me."

The ground was soggy from the drizzle. Jack didn't patronize the gravel pathways. He knew the place well enough to take all the shortcuts through the mud.

The Despardieu family tomb was creamy, veined marble, and beautifully maintained. Two fluted columns framed the inscription plaque. A winged angel, eyes closed in ecstasy, played a lyre overhead. The tomb was set off by a wrought-iron fence, the kind that ran around the balconies of the finer houses in the French Quarter. On the narrow walkway around the tomb, crushed seashells substituted for

157

gravel. Breaux opened the gate with a key from a huge bunch attached to his belt.

"Always keep it locked?" Spraggue asked.

"Yeah. 'Course I can't say what the policy was when that skeleton come aboard. I been here seven, eight years, that's all. Guys from the Coroner's Office, ones that took the pictures an' all, they seem to t'ink our extra stiff came here long before me."

"Exactly what happened that day?"

"We were short-staffed, like usual, or a lotta t'ings woulda happen different. When we prep a place, we usually do it the day before, right, but we couldn't get it done, so we tried for the mornin' of the funeral. See, that's where the trouble was. We woulda had enough time, okay. There wouldn'a been no trouble wit' time, 'cause all we hadda do was burn the ol' wood coffin an' brush the bones back in the pit. We check the date on the oven we gonna open, an' that is fine. No action at that tomb fo' six years—no action on this vault for almos' twenny, see. We figure no trouble. Jus' bones after that long."

"Six years and twenty years?"

"See right here." Breaux pointed to the tablet blockin' the door to the lower oven. "This one been sealed up fo' six years. Hope they don' make us open it an' see if there's jus' one body in it. This top one's where the extra body was—an' the las' time it was open was fo' the eart'ly remains a Miss Evelyn Despardieu, on February 12, 1966. Nineteen years ago, right?"

"Go on."

"I was the one made the discovery. Me an' Henry Wayne, we workin' a little quick-like, 'cause of the family's gonna come out at two in the afternoon, see, an' we wanna set out a few chairs for the old folks an' such. We ain't worried 'bout nothin'. All we got to do is remove the marble plate an' straighten out the matter of the remains."

"How do you remove the plate?"

"Well, it ain't too hard. You jus' chip the mortar away,

158

bein' careful not t' bung up the marble. Wrap a clot' 'round it, an' use a good chisel, an' you home free. Takes a while, but it ain't hard. After the plate's gone, the door's jus' bricked up, an' you can bang away pretty good. Bricks don' matter. Cheap.''

"Sounds noisy."

"Hammer an' chisel make a good noise, yeah. But the neighbors don' complain, eh?''

"Is somebody always on guard here?'' Spraggue asked.

"Oh, yeah. You bet, *cher*. If you're t'inkin' that somebody jus' come by an' open a vault an' nobody heard him, you're plenty wrong.''

"What do you think happened?''

"This is jus' my opinion, you know.'' Breaux drained his coffee cup and set it on the edge of the tomb. "Cops didn't want my opinion none, and neither did the press.''

"I'd like to hear your opinion,'' Spraggue said.

Breaux brightened and hitched up his coveralls. "Okay. I'd say the two skeletons was put in together. Like, if ol' Miss Despardieu was young Miss Despardieu—you know, eighteen an' gorgeous an' sexy an' all—an' killed in some car crash, I'd say her boyfriend jus' sneaked in here the night after the funeral and killed hisself to be wit' her.''

A graveyard romantic. Spraggue wondered if Breaux was familiar with *Romeo and Juliet*. Or *Hamlet*. *How long will a man lie i' th' earth ere he rot?*

"You think the extra person died here?'' Spraggue asked. "Killed himself?''

"I reckon.''

"How did he close the tomb up afterward?''

"Oh. Well, I don' know how they used t' do it. But sometimes, if we gotta lot to do, we jus' lean the tablet up 'gainst the oven, an' brick it up the next day or so. Caretakers woulda just bricked it up. No reason to look inside.''

"That's not unusual?''

"Not a bit.''

"Okay. Go on."

"Well, it was the damnedest t'ing. Gimme the creeps, ı guarantee. I open up the tomb, an' there's this skeleton, jus' lyin' flat out next t' the coffin. You know what it made me t'ink of? Buried alive. I mean I t'ought the ol' gal, somehow, she gets up outta the coffin, an' she couldn' get outta the tomb. Who's that ol' gal who's buried wit' her telephone so she can call everybody when the final trumpet sounds? Well, I t'ought maybe Miss Despardieu got outta her coffin, an' it made me feel all creepy, an' usually I don' feel like that none. So we didn' call the cops right away, or call the church even, 'cause we t'ought it was Miss Despardieu's remains. We didn' holler till we broke open the coffin and found the other corpse. Even then we t'ought 'bout it a little. Henry's all for jus' pushin' the extra bones in the caveau. He t'ought it's jus' some member a the family got careless treatment last time 'round. But it didn' look right to me, no. I mean, the guy's wearin' rags a blue jeans, not what people are mostly buried in. And, well, the whole t'ing jus' wasn't right—an' it was kinda scary, you bet."

"You were right to call the police," Spraggue said when Breaux paused and shook his head.

"Well, I don' know. They weren' too happy 'bout it. I mean, they got more importan' t'ings to do than trace an ol' stiff. But you gotta wonder who he was—an' how come nobody miss him. What kind a guy is it that nobody misses?"

"You sure it was a man?"

"Lot bigger than Miss Despardieu. Coroner'll be able t' tell you more than me. All I can say is he didn' have no money in his pockets, didn' have no wallet or nothin'."

"Nothing at all?" Spraggue asked, noticing an uncharacteristic hesitation in the man's voice.

"Well, I guess the cops'll tell you, if you ask," Breaux said, fingering the pocket where he'd stashed the ten-dollar bill.

160

"You think it's worth more?" Spraggue asked.

"Me, how would I know a t'ing like that?" Breaux smiled broadly, showing stained tombstone teeth.

Spraggue parted with another ten. He got more than he expected.

Twenty

Breaux allowed a single phone call from his shack.
Rawlins was back at the station.

"I've got something," Spraggue said quickly. "Can you
meet me at the Coroner's Office?"

"Your aunt's comin' by in a few minutes," the detective
said, sounding pleased about it.

"Bring her along," Spraggue said. "She's not squeam-
ish."

The coroner's waiting room was an oddly shaped, par-
titioned section of a larger room, featuring a public telephone in the far corner, two doors leading off to lavatories,
a battered sofa, and two metal chairs. A framed motto on
one cracked off-white wall read, "Where death delights to
serve the living." It was the only attempt at decoration.
The place smelled like a hospital ward.

The coroner provided while-you-wait reading material in
the form of a stack of yellow cards, headed THESE ARE
CORONER CASES. About half the words on each card were
typed in boldface. Spraggue had gotten as far as "**all cases
of alleged rape, simple and aggravated, carnal knowl-**

edge and crimes **against nature,**" when he heard his aunt approaching.

Her voice was raised and argumentative, and got louder as she came up the stairs. "This man, Renner," she was saying, "is probably certifiable."

The door lurched open and she entered, wrapped in a shiny yellow slicker. Rawlins followed, pausing in the doorway to shake off a huge black umbrella.

"You made good time," Spraggue said, motioning them both into the waiting room. "First, tell me about Renner and then I'll tell you what I've got."

Rawlins helped Mary out of her raincoat. It dripped a pattern of dots onto the linoleum floor.

"Archibald Renner," Mary said firmly, "was a great disappointment to me. Brother Archibald, I should call him. That's what he calls himself. I had imagined some grim, austere cleric, and instead I got Friar Tuck. Archie Renner is fatter than Friar Tuck. He has something wrong with one foot, and wears a very noticeably built-up shoe. He could no more have made an unnoticed appearance at that banquet, disguised as a waiter or a cook, than I could pass for Sophia Loren."

"He could have hired someone," Rawlins said.

"Oh, Rawl." The argument was about to start again. "If you could have seen him! So awkward and silly and sort of lost. An adult child—"

"Okay, okay," Rawlins said. "He's a washout." He turned to Spraggue and said, "Tell me what you've got."

"I'll show you," Spraggue said.

With Rawlins' shield to intimidate the smiling but hostile receptionist, they zipped past the administrative desks in the lobby and got clear through to a comfortable office furnished with a huge, old-fashioned walnut desk and leather furniture. Tanks of tropical fish burbled along one wall. Spraggue had expected an old man to be coroner— the very word seemed to summon a vision of the faithful family doctor, side-whiskered and bespectacled. The white-coated man behind the desk looked like a first-year medical student, possibly an undergraduate. When he smiled, the tiny crinkles under his eyes made Spraggue think that he might be old enough to get served in a bar.

Dr. Noonan was excited and enthusiastic, which meant he hadn't been on the job long. His freshness made Spraggue feel jaded.

He also had the gift of concentrating completely on the issue at hand. Once his interest was piqued, he shoved away a mound of paperwork, sat back in his swivel chair, and really listened.

"Yeah," he said, tapping a pencil on his blotter, "that's kind of a neat one, a neat case, you know. I haven't had that much chance to play with old bones, and these are like a gift, being as how nothing's known about who they came from. I got a chance to do tests I'd only read about in books before. I'll be glad to tell you about them, but let me get the file. I hate to trust my memory. I get the cases mixed up."

Dr. Noonan's white coat had a nameplate on the breast pocket. *Dr. G. Noonan.*

"Now all this stuff is 'iffy,' if you know what I mean," the coroner said, pulling papers triumphantly from a filing cabinet. "Approximate. I hollered for help on this one, called in a forensic pathologist from Tulane. We got enough so that if you ask me, 'Is this the body of Judge Crater?' I can say, definitely, no. But if you ask me to pick out an identity for our guy, say from a list of all the people who disappeared between the years 1960 and 1970, I can't really help you. You get me a name and a set of dental records, and I can tell you if they match."

"Could we whittle down that list of missing persons?" Spraggue asked. "Eliminate the women? Narrow it down by height, by age . . ."

"Sure," Noonan said. "Height is easy. That's just measuring a thigh bone and looking it up in a table. This

164

guy fits into your average group, though. Not much help. He's five foot ten. He was."

"Age?"

"We determine age by the hardness of the skull, and the formations on the top of it, which put our man in his late twenties, early thirties. So far he fits your profile of a standard murder victim."

"How did he get killed?"

"I can show you that, if you'd like."

Spraggue could recognize an enthusiast when he saw one. Rawlins glanced questioningly at Mary, but she eagerly accepted the invitation.

The autopsy room and the morgue were in the basement, two large connecting squares, cool and smelling faintly of dampness, strongly of disinfectant. Two walls of the morgue were comprised of refrigerated units, divided into drawers. The floor was blotchy linoleum, stained and scrubbed colorless. In the next room, the floor of the autopsy room was white tile, with central drainage. Two rectangular steel tables were spotlighted by arching overhead beams. One corner held a forklift. Another was filled with scales and weights.

Spraggue found himself taking inventory of what he'd eaten recently. As a precaution, he switched from "real person" to "actor," excising himself neatly from the scene. This had nothing to do with him. It was scripted, fantasy. He could turn the lights on at any time. He was still in control. He wished.

Dr. Noonan stopped near one of the drawers so suddenly that his shoes made a skidding sound on the linoleum.

"We're playing it by the book," he said solemnly. "Even though we don't think there'll be any relatives to identify the bones, we decided we'd better put them in a viewing drawer, just like any other body. He's not much to look at, but better than some we get. Not so fresh as some, but a lot fresher than others. He's been dead so long he doesn't even stink."

Rawl made a face, but Mary came closer, fascinated.

The skeleton seemed so small, so diminished, in a drawer designed for holding a body. It had been partially wired together. The torso and pelvis were connected, the ribs in place. Leg and arm bones were appropriately placed, but totally separate from the trunk. The teeth were shocking, so white and prominent.

"He was on his back," Noonan said, referring to his notes. "Laid out sort of for burial, except that he was on top of the coffin instead of in it. Damp as it is in Louisiana, his organs and fleshy parts would have rotted away in a couple of years, and he's been dead a lot longer than that."

"How long?"

"Over fifteen years."

"What killed him?" Rawlins asked. He spoke in a normal tone, but the hush of the place magnified it, made it echo.

"Well," Noonan said, "this man could have been shot to death and the bullet could have passed through the body without striking a bone. He could have been stabbed. He could have been poisoned with some arcane substance. If he'd been strangled, I probably would have found a broken hyoid bone."

"Could he have just died?" Mary asked. "Of the proverbial natural causes?"

Noonan had gloves on his hands, thin plastic gloves so tight they disappeared against his skin, leaving his hands shiny. He touched the skeleton now, turning the skull, displaying a fissure in the back, near the right side.

"He didn't die any natural death," he said. "Not with this crack in his skull. He wouldn't have been walking around with this."

"That little crack is enough to cause death?" Rawl peered into the drawer. His hand went out as if to touch the bones, then drew back.

"A blow strong enough to cause that crack would have done a great deal of damage. You don't crack your skull by knocking your head against a wall. A lot of force was applied to this guy's head."

Rawlins paced slowly to the other side of the room. "This is all damned interestin'," he said, nodding to Spraggue to join him over in the far corner while Noonan readjusted the bones and closed the drawer. "But I don't see what the hell it has to do with Joe Fontenot."

"Hang on," Spraggue said. He turned back to Noonan. "What was found on the skeleton in the way of clothing? Odds and ends?"

" 'Odds and ends' is good. Cloth has its own rotting cycle. Cotton goes fast, linen lasts longer, nylon and synthetics stick around quite a while. We sent the stuff to the FBI forensic lab. They're good, but slow."

"Could we see the articles?" Spraggue asked.

"Sure. I'd say they'd be back from Atlanta in a couple of weeks, probably."

"A couple of weeks!" Spraggue echoed.

"This guy has been dead a while," Noonan said defensively. "I couldn't exactly put a priority rush on it."

"Was there any unusual object found with the bones?" Spraggue asked.

"Unusual . . . Now, let me think. Yeah, yeah. I remember. I don't even have to look it up. One of those leather bags full of mumbo jumbo. We find them on a lot of corpses. Mostly blacks, but a few whites. This one was a real good one, I'd say. Seemed old. Fine leather bag."

"A fine leather bag . . ." Rawlins repeated.

"You think you know who the skeleton is? Who it might be?" Dr. Noonan's enthusiasm made him look even more like a gawky, excited teenager.

"I think we have to talk," Rawlins said to Spraggue.

"Dr. Noonan," Mary said, flashing her most tactful smile, "you have been so helpful. Is there somewhere the three of us could go to have a little private discussion?"

"I'll go get a cup of coffee," Noonan said, polite but wistful. "I could use one. But," he turned and looked back from the doorway, "I sure would like to know what's going on."

"So would I," Rawlins said as soon as the coroner's footsteps petered out. "You're connecting this skeleton to Fontenot because both of 'em had a gris-gris bag?"

"This particular gris-gris bag is not something you buy in the five-and-dime. It's special, the sort you'd get if you asked for protection for a dangerous undertaking, like going off to war—or robbing a Brink's truck."

"How do you know so much about it?"

Aunt Mary raised her eyes warningly to the ceiling, and Spraggue said, "Look, let me tell you a story. A lot of it's conjecture, but it fits the facts."

"Go ahead," Rawlins said with a sigh. "What can it hurt?" There was one folding chair in the corner. He jerked it open and offered the seat to Mary.

"Here goes," Spraggue said. "Stop me if I go too fast. Three people pulled the Morgan City robbery. One of them was Fontenot. Fontenot was in New Orleans up to the time of the crime, living with Dora. So it's fairly safe to assume that the other two robbers were also in New Orleans. Okay so far?"

"Okay."

"The robbery occurs, and gets out of hand. Fontenot is caught. This is on February 5, 1966. One week later, February 12, 1966, Miss Evelyn Despardieu is buried, along with an extra body."

"Now you've lost me," Rawlins said.

"If you were going to pull a tricky holdup with two other people, wouldn't you pick a place to meet to split up the dough afterward? Maybe you'd even wait a week for things to cool off."

"Maybe, but why the hell would I pick some graveyard for the meetin'? What connection is there between that graveyard and Fontenot?"

"Remember," Spraggue said to Mary, "what Dora told me when I asked about her husband's work?"

168

"She said he was unemployed most of the time."

"Yeah, and she said that sometimes he'd come home all dirty, as if he'd taken a job doing construction. And he didn't like to talk about it. And he seemed down on those occasions, even though he'd have a little money for the rent. And sometimes he'd bring home flowers on those days, all sorts of flowers, from florists, some that looked like they'd been picked along the road, like you might get in a graveyard."

Mary brightened. "You think he worked part-time at the cemetery?"

"I think one of the gang did. Maybe Fontenot helped out his buddy who worked there every once in a while."

"Go on," Rawlins said.

"Let's say the two robbers meet in the graveyard. There's a fight, and one of them dies. A tomb is open and ready. The caretaker at the cemetery said it's not unusual for a vault to get bricked up the day after a funeral. In goes the extra body."

"Let's say that," Rawlins agreed. "Where does it get us?"

"It gets us a dead body in a secret grave, one very rich killer, and James French, also known as Joe Fontenot, in jail."

"Okay."

"Now skip to French's release. What does he do, first thing, this man who's held his tongue and patiently waited for his reward?"

"He contacts his fellow thieves," Mary said promptly. "And demands his rightful share."

Spraggue smiled. "Yeah. And does the thief and killer say, 'Here you go. Here's your share. There's more for you because I knocked off the third guy?'"

"I don't know what he'd say," Rawlins offered. "But I'm sure you've got some idea."

"Well, he might say, 'Joe, I don't know how to break this to you, but we were both deceived. Our third partner never showed up at the graveyard that night. He had all the money, and he took off and left us high and dry. I've been searching for the bastard ever since, but he must have changed his name and skipped the country. Can you imagine cheating your friends like that?' ''

"And Fontenot believed him," Mary murmured.

"Until he saw an article in the newspaper," Spraggue said. "And the article turned his life around."

Rawlins ran his hands through his hair. "Let me get this straight. You're saying that Fontenot was blackmailin' one of his former partners."

"Right after this article came out," Spraggue said, "Fontenot made a down payment on a restaurant. He started collecting big money every month."

"Can we prove any of this?" Rawlins asked.

"We can find out if Fontenot made inquiries about this article—at the newspaper, at the police station, at the cemetery."

"Okay," Rawlins said.

"And somebody can find out what kind of employment records they keep for graveyard workers."

"I'll do that," Mary said. "What do I look for?"

"A man who worked there in 'sixty-five or 'sixty-six, and left in February of 'sixty-six."

"Not much," Rawlins said.

"His first name was Robert, and his last name was probably something French."

"Oh?" Rawlins said.

"Jeannine Fontenot told me her husband got a windfall legacy from his old friend, T-Bob. She said T-Bob and Joe were two of the three musketeers—"

Footsteps interrupted him.

"Sorry," Dr. Noonan said. "Can you pick up the phone, Sergeant Rawlins? It's your office, and they say it's urgent."

A white wall phone blended into the surrounding tile so

thoroughly it was practically invisible. Dr. Noonan had to point it out.

"Rawlins here," the detective rasped. An expression of sheer incredulity spread across his face. "She's where? She what?" He nodded and grunted, said, "Hang on. I'll be right there," and slammed the receiver down.

"Damn." The word exploded out of him.

"What?"

"It's no good. I gotta get back to my office. Dora Levoyer just confessed to the murder of Joseph Fontenot."

Twenty-One

Rawlins edged out of the homicide lieutenant's office as gracefully as a man with half the belly, and slammed the door hard enough to shake the partitions dividing up the squad room.

Spraggue stopped pacing the worn brown rug. "She's lying. Let me talk to her."

"She ain't in there."

"Where did they take her?"

"No place."

The sergeant banged his clenched fist against the drawer of a tan filing cabinet. "I can't believe this," he said. "I'm off chasing theories and in she comes, leavin' a note, addressed to me personal, confessin' to the whole shebang. And then she waltzes out the door."

"She's not here?" Spraggue said.

"That's what I'm telling you."

"What did the note say?"

"I'm out tryin' to clear her name and in she comes and—"

"*What did it say?*"

"Christ, hang on. I made a copy. Here, read it yourself, and don't try tell me it ain't a confession."

To whom it may concern, the note began. It was handwritten. The Xerox machine had botched the raised Imperial Orleans logo and the cheap white paper didn't come close to matching the quality of the creamy hotel stationery. *I stabbed Joseph Fontenot. I regret the trouble I have caused.* It was signed *Dora Levoyer.*

"We compared it with samples of her writing," Rawlins said. "So don't go thinkin'—"

"She wrote it," Spraggue said.

"I'm gonna hate tellin' your aunt about this."

"How long has she been gone? Anybody see her leave?"

"Sergeant Hayes saw her comin' out of the office, tried to stop her. She walked right over him practically, and Hayes is one big guy. Said she looked real out-of-it and that worried him some, so he went by the office and saw the note. Figured he'd better check it out even if it had my name on it. Called me right after."

"She can't have been gone more than twenty minutes."

"Fifteen, twenty minutes, yeah."

"Mr. Spraggue! Michael!" The shout came from across the room. Pierce's voice was barely recognizable, it was so different from his normal dignified murmur. A uniformed man was trying to hang on to one of the butler's arms, but Pierce was making progress, practically dragging the uniform across the floor.

"Let him go," Rawlins barked. "What is this?"

"Dora." Pierce was breathing hard. He tried to recapture his dignity by smoothing back his hair. "She's gone. She left this." He stuck his hand out, offering a stiff Imperial Orleans envelope. "I couldn't reach you. I thought the police . . ."

The envelope was ripped open across the top. Spraggue skimmed the message. Same stuff. I did it. I'm sorry.

Pierce kept talking. "She was in her room, knitting, not less than an hour ago. Humming the way she does. We

173

had coffee. She hardly ate anything. She asked if I thought Mrs. Hillman would mind if she worked in the Imperial Orleans kitchen until the case came to trial. Denise had invited her—''

''She talked to Denise?''

''Not today. Earlier. Yesterday, the day before—''

''She get any phone calls? Anything? Letters?''

''A phone call. There was a call while I was washing up. But it was a wrong number.''

''Dora said it was a wrong number?''

The butler nodded.

''Was she upset by the call?''

''It's hard to tell with Dora.'' Pierce passed a hand over his forehead. ''She went back to her room. I made phone calls—your aunt had asked me to. To brokers. I did that, answered mail, then ordered dinner. Dora was in her room with the door open. Knitting, humming. Then her door was closed. Maybe an hour later, I don't know, I was uneasy somehow. No humming. She was gone. The note was on her pillow. You don't think—''

''The phone call was the only interruption. Is there a phone in Dora's room?''

''Yes, but . . . No, it wasn't the only interruption. You had a visitor. A young woman. Striking. Dark hair. She said to tell you—let me see, I wrote it down . . .'' Pierce scrabbled for the piece of scrap paper in his pants pocket. ''She said she'd taken something you wanted from her mother's house. She wouldn't leave a name or address or number. She laughed, and said you could figure it out.''

''While Dora was there?''

''In her room.''

''With the door open? Think.''

''I think so. I don't know. I just don't know.''

''Rawlins,'' Spraggue said. ''Was Dora alone? When she came in here?''

''I didn't ask. I think Hayes woulda mentioned—''

''Have Mary wait for me here.''

174

"I don't wanna be the one to tell her—"

"Show her the notes. Get an APB out for Dora."

"Where you goin'?"

"Aimee Fontenot's."

Twenty-Two

Since Flowers had driven Aunt Mary to St. Louis, Number Three, where the Office of Cemeteries was located, Spraggue hailed a cab to take him to Aimee Fontenot's apartment. The driver was silent and sullen under a checked cloth cap, but he knew the city and avoided the worst of the road construction on the way.

Was it only yesterday morning he had stood here, angrily jabbing the buzzer marked "Fontenot" and getting no response? Time seemed compressed, days dense with movement. He was beyond tiredness, his body surging with the opening-night adrenaline that carried him through the rush of performance. There was no leisure to debate or argue the right course. Just the scene to be played, the clue to be followed, the single path to trace through a morass of menacing roads.

No wait this time. Footsteps on the stairs. Aimee didn't trust the buzzer that admitted people to the building. He saw her through the door's dirty window pane and was bowled over again by the sheer vitality of Joe Fontenot's daughter. Even through a haze of dusty glass, she seemed painted in brighter colors, with bolder strokes, than the rest of humanity.

"Come on in," she said, and there was no come-hither in her voice. She seemed younger even than her years, strangely subdued, as if she had made some decision that had left her numb, beyond play-acting. She wore a white cotton shirt, open at the neck and way too large—a man's shirt—and tiny blue cotton shorts that barely edged out beneath the shirt. Her feet were bare. Gone was the green paint on toenails and fingertips. She looked defenseless without it.

Her apartment was as strange and colorful as she was. Pale stripped wood and blotches of bright primary color, wild and primitive. One room held all her possessions, and it was uncrowded. A mattress on the floor, covered with a red Indian print bedspread, acted as both couch and bed. A stained and battered rag doll sat on the pillow. Bright paper lanterns covered the bare-lightbulb fixtures. One wall was decorated with Mardi Gras masks: hawks, eagles, lions, and wolves, feathered and sequined, watched over the room. The effect was garish, playful—and threatening. Contradictory, like Aimee Fontenot. Innocent and experienced. Young and old. On the make one minute, defensive the next.

"There's a folding chair in the closet, if you want it," she said.

"I can sit on the floor."

"You're not too old for that?" she said, with some of the harshness creeping back into her voice.

"I'll sit on the bed," Spraggue said. "Okay?"

"Okay," she muttered.

She sank cross-legged to the wooden floor and rested her elbows on her knees, cupping her chin in her palms.

"Pierce said you had something for me."

"The snobby guy who answered your door? Is he your servant or something?"

"He works for my aunt."

"How nice for her." Her fingers traced a crack in the floorboards. "I took some stuff out of the house last night. Put it in the trunk of my car before you broke in."

"So you were the mysterious burglar who got there first."

"Yeah. The papers in the drawer were just recipes and junk. I took them and I took some personal shit, things I wanted to look through without my mother hanging over my neck—"

"But now your conscience is tormenting you," Spraggue said flatly, "and you want to give them to me."

"Yeah." Her voice was scarcely more than a whisper.

"Why not sell them? You were all hot to cut a deal last night."

She stared at her unadorned nails. "They're not for sale."

"Staring at your baby pictures got you all sentimental, right?"

"You shut up! Maybe it did. I don't expect you to understand. Maybe it made me remember a time when I was . . ." The anger melted out of her voice and left it quiet. "Different," she finished lamely. "Just different. And people loved me." She stood in a single motion, grabbed a pile of books off a cardboard box, and dropped them at his feet. "Take this shit and get out."

The leather bindings were sprinkled with flaking gold-leaf fleurs-de-lys. They held thick yellowing pages. Spraggue opened one at random. Six square photos to the page. Black-and-white. "This your dog?" he asked to break the silence.

"I don't want your goddamn pity. I don't want a thing you're selling."

"It would help if you'd show me some pictures."

"Why?"

"Something your mother said, about your dad's old friends. One was a guy named T-Bob—"

"I never met him," she said. "Mom used to talk about

him. Dad, too. I don't think they were friends though. I think Joe hated him for something.''

"Could you show me a picture of T-Bob?"

"Maybe. Mom captioned some of the pictures. I can at least show you the right book to look in.''

"When you went to my hotel room," Spraggue said, his eyes searching Aimee's face, "did you notice a woman there?''

Aimee turned away. "She stared at me, stared at me like I was, I don't know, a ghost or something. I got out of there fast.''

She picked up the photo albums and plumped herself down on the mattress next to Spraggue. Yesterday, she had seemed like a hooker with thirty years' experience. Today, she was a high school girl who'd never been kissed.

They began with the book he'd leafed through that first morning, while Albert Flowers had taken photos downstairs.

"This is Mom. Not much older than I am now. I don't look like her, do I? But you can tell I'm Joe's daughter. This is Gran'mere. She died when I was three, maybe. Gran'pere, when I was four. These were all taken way before I was born. Mom wasn't half as good-looking when she was young. She knows how to put herself together now. Back then, they were so damned poor, she made all her clothes and stuff. Mine, too." She shook her head. "I guess you wouldn't know anything about that.''

"I didn't live your life. You didn't live mine.''

"Here." She pointed at a fuzzy shot. "That's my dad gone fishing with two guys. One of them could be T-Bob, I suppose. They're all about the same age.''

"You have a magnifying glass?''

"Nope.''

Spraggue stared at the photo. Three men grinned back at him, squinting against sunshine. The two sidemen pointed at a fish in a net held by the man in the middle. Spraggue thought Fontenot was the one in the center, but

179

the graininess of the photo was such that he couldn't be sure. He slipped it out of its black photo-corners. No names on the back. Maybe with a magnifying glass—maybe Mrs. Fontenot could identify the men.

"Can I take this one?" he asked. "You'll get it back."

"Here's Momma and Gran'mere," Aimee said. "You can burn any pictures of Joe."

She flipped a page and Jeannine Fontenot disappeared from the photos. The first page had been mostly Jeannine, posing in a bathing suit, laughing, hiding behind a tree. Then the album switched focus, the pages taken up by photos of Aimee as a child.

No photos of Jeannine pregnant.

And now, no photos of Joe Fontenot at all.

"Oh," Aimee said, "look at these." It was an early birthday party. A three-year-old Aimee beamed out from the photos. Her grin lit up the page.

She rubbed her fingertips over the smooth surfaces of the photos. Some of the hardness seemed to wash away from her eyes, and Spraggue saw why she hadn't asked for money. She was trying to live up to that child, to that impossible, unblemished promise.

In one of the birthday photos, a man dandled her on his knee.

"Is that your father?" Spraggue pointed, peering hard. He thought he knew the man, but the image was so small, and slightly blurred.

"My dad? I didn't have a dad until I was seven years old. Learning to cook fancy was more important than raising a daughter." A hint of the old bitterness was there, but she was still lost in a long-ago world. She held the photo up to a blue-shaded lightbulb. "I think, yeah, I think that's Uncle Paulie. I remember him. Momma said I used to call him Papa, and she always had to set me straight. I haven't thought about him in years. Uncle Paulie. Yeah. I wonder what happened to him . . ."

"Can I use your phone?"

"For twenty cents, it's yours. That's for a local call."
She paid no further attention to him, as she leaned back on
the bed, searching through the pages of her past.

He asked for Rawlins, got Hayes. Requested Pierce,
found Aunt Mary.

"Darling." Her voice came over the line after several
clicks that made him think he'd been cut off. "I found it.
At the Office of Cemeteries."

"T-Bob?"

"I hope so. It was tricky. They keep more detailed records about the dead people, the people buried in the cemetery, than about the live people who worked there. But a
Robert Landry was hired in the summer of 'sixty-five. Does
that sound like the one we're looking for?"

"Could be."

"Is Dora with you?"

"No."

"Oh, dear, I was hoping—There's something else,
something more important."

"What?"

"Another name on the records, another man who worked
part-time at the graveyard."

"Paul Armand?" Spragg said.

"Paul Armand," Mary said at the same time.

"Look, let me talk to Rawlins."

"He's right here."

"Does he know about Armand?"

"I just got here."

"Put him on."

The detective drawled his name into the phone. "Got
anything?"

"Yes."

"We got a bit ourselves. Seems your cook didn't leave
alone. Desk sergeant staring out the window saw her get
in the passenger side of a brown Buick."

"Shit."

"We got the airport and the bus station and the train depot watched."

"Forget about them. Check out the driver's license on Paul Armand. I'll bet you find he's got a Buick."

"Armand?"

"Mary'll tell you about it. Get some people over to his restaurant, find out where he lives, and send somebody over there—"

"You'll meet us at the restaurant?"

"I guess." Spraggue hung up, turned around to say a quick good-bye to Aimee, and stopped with the words half out of his mouth.

He knew where they would go.

He whirled and snatched the phone out of the cradle, dialed Rawlins' office. The *beep-beep-beep* of the busy signal blared in his ear.

Twenty-Three

All the cabs in the city had disappeared. Spraggue ran, sweating in the late afternoon steambath, tripping over the uneven cobblestone sidewalks of the *Vieux Carré*. He spotted a taxi cruising Dauphine and practically jumped in front of it to force it to a halt.

"Imperial Orleans." He was surprised at how calm his voice sounded. Sweat trickled in a thin line down his chest.

At the corner of Conti, he shoved a twenty into the cabbie's hand, coupled with instructions and the promise of another twenty to come.

Two and a half blocks to run.

The hotel's banquet rooms were on the second floor. The thickly carpeted stairway muffled his racing footsteps.

The door from the hallway to the display room was sealed with a gold police sticker. Maybe he was wrong. No. He *knew*, knew the last act, knew where the leading man would have to play the final scene. The entrance to the larger banquet room swung open easily. An ornate white door broke the line of the far wall. Its police sticker hung limply from the jamb.

Spraggue crossed the room, paused with his hand on the doorknob, listened for voices within.

Wait for Rawlins?

He couldn't take the chance.

He opened the door a crack and edged in, silent on thick gold carpet.

The room was as it had been the night of the murder. Spraggue felt he'd already seen it through Mary's eyes, the hanging pots and pans, the glistening displays of cookware, all frozen in place since the police had sealed it off. The chandeliers overhead cast dim shadows in spite of the afternoon light that filtered through the gauze curtains.

At first he thought the room was empty. So many rows of tables. Such absolute silence. The room might have been in the middle of a cemetery, on an island. His own breathing sounded harsh and ragged.

"Go away." He heard Dora's voice before he saw her and whipped around to locate the sound, relief flooding through him as he turned. "Go away," Dora pleaded.

"You," was all the man said. Spraggue didn't have to hear the voice to identify the speaker. Uncle Paulie. Paul Armand.

Spraggue could see two figures in the fading light, one seated, one standing. He was sure they were close to a white outline on the floor, near the tape that marked where Fontenot's body had been found. Dora's suicide would play best there.

"Dora," he called. "Are you okay?"

"Go away." All her energy was directed into those two words.

"He's been lying to you, Dora."

"Enough of that," Armand said.

"What did he tell you to make you write that confession?"

"Shut up."

"It was my idea, *monsieur*, all my idea."

184

"Did he tell you Aimee killed Fontenot? That your daughter killed her father?"

"It's better left unsaid. Please, *monsieur*, I've made my choice. She will not come to me if she hears strange voices. Leave me, please."

"She's not coming here. I just left her."

"You saw her? You know?" Dora's voice sounded strange and sleepy. She was the seated figure. Her head lolled from side to side.

Dammit. The last act had already started. He'd missed the curtain.

"He gave you something to drink, didn't he, Dora?"

She laughed. It echoed through the room and ended on a long lazy sigh. "I know I should not drink in the afternoon. So sleepy."

"Get up, Dora," Spraggue said. "Get up and walk over here. I'll take you to your daughter."

"Oh, *monsieur*, I'm so tired. Can't she come here? Monsieur Armand said she wished to see me. I told him she owes me nothing, no explanation . . ."

Something glittered in Armand's hand. "She's not going anywhere," he said.

"Your daughter didn't kill Fontenot, Dora. Armand killed him."

"*Non, monsieur*. My daughter, I saw my daughter. She came to the hotel room. So beautiful, my daughter—"

"Quiet!" Armand poised his knife behind Dora's shoulder. She didn't seem to notice it. Were her eyes closed or open? "Did Jeannine tell you?"

"Jeannine, Dora, Aimee. They all told me," Spraggue said. "Jeannine, married for five childless years in a place that doesn't exactly preach birth control. Jeannine, so protective of her only child. Dora, convinced that her baby didn't die at birth, certain she made arrangements with some kindly nurse to have the baby adopted, raised in a good Catholic home. Aimee told me herself, that little girl

185

in the photographs told me, the one with Uncle Paulie, not papa. Is your wife still a maternity nurse?''

"Speak more slowly.'' Dora shook her head as if she were trying to clear it. ''I don't understand—''

"Shut up,'' Armand said. "Stay in your chair and go to sleep. You know you want to go to sleep.''

"What did you put in her drink?''

"Enough.'' The knife glittered.

Time. How much time did he have? Enough to wait for Rawlins and the police to catch up? Dora wasn't unconscious yet. Would Armand have risked drugging her before her stroll into the police station?

Spraggue took a step forward.

"Don't come any closer.''

"How did you work the adoption?'' What if the cabbie didn't go to the police? *Time.* Maybe it was bringing Rawlins closer, but every minute took Dora farther away.

Spraggue's eyes had adjusted to the dimness. He could see Armand smile. The chef was wearing a striped short-sleeved shirt, dark pants, a dark tie. He looked less dignified, older minus his tall toque. The knife in his hand seemed a natural extension of one bony arm. He gestured with it and said, "It doesn't matter.''

"Then why not tell me?''

"Why not?'' Armand licked dry lips. The knife was a slicing blade, maybe six inches long. Spraggue's eyes checked the periphery of the room. Where was the knife display? "It'll pass the time,'' Armand said. "We've got time. Unless you told the police?''

"No,'' Spraggue lied.

"And why not? Why the hell not?'' The knife moved closer to Dora's cheek.

"Because of Aimee,'' Spraggue said quickly, "and Dora. If Dora wants to tell her, that's one thing, but it's none of the cops' business, right?''

Armand seemed satisfied for the moment. Spraggue

thought that he never sounded quite so truthful as when he lied. Actor tricks.

"We were old friends," Armand said, so softly Spragge could barely hear. "Joe and me . . ."

"And T-Bob."

Armand's chin snapped up when he heard the name. "How did you know about—"

"Believe me," Spragge said. "I know. I'm not here because of T-Bob or Fontenot. I'm not here because of the past. I'm here for Dora."

"She's just about asleep."

"Go on, tell me about the adoption." *Hurry up, Rawlins.*

Armand licked his lips again, kept his voice low. "It's my one good deed," he said, "and I suppose it won't go unpunished. I did it out of friendship. Believe it or not, I did it out of love. Joe was my pal. I cared for Joe, but more than that, I cared for Jeannine. I loved her. If Joe hadn't married her, I woulda married her so fast . . . She was unhappy back then. Lord, unhappy doesn't say half. Her sisters all had children, her in-laws never gave her a moment's peace. It was painful to watch her, to watch what she was turning into, to see her change, get so desperate, so obsessed. There was nothin' else she wanted in the world but a baby. She wanted to adopt, but she was so scared that Joe would never love the kid, that he would leave her. She thought he'd leave her anyway because she couldn't have a baby. And he did."

"Wait, please, a minute." Dora's voice was soft and slurred. "I don't understand. What is—"

"Shut up!"

"Jeannine told me he was a cook in Paris," Spragge said quickly. He hoped the police wouldn't use sirens. Nothing to alarm the man who clutched the knife so tightly, inches from Dora's face.

"Oh, yeah." Armand snorted. "A fancy cook in Paris. Nothin' but fantasy. He walked out. He never intended to go back. I know. I was here in New Orleans, already married myself, when Joe took up with this one." He jabbed the blade in Dora's direction. "Lookin' back, sometimes I think Joe was just waitin' for me to marry before he left Jeannine. He didn't want her, without kids, but he didn't want me to have her, kids or no. Anyhow, he took up with Dora here. I can't say it was true love on his part. He was lonely. He used a different name because—well, something happened, and—"

"A robbery happened. The robbery of an armored van in Morgan City. One man was killed. A man was captured."

It was cool in the vast room, but Spraggue thought he could see beads of sweat at Armand's hairline, gathering, rolling down his seamed face. The chef nodded at Dora.

"She's asleep," he said. "Joe never knew she was pregnant. And after he—well, after he went away, I watched. I felt responsible. I'd told Joe, if anything happened . . . Well . . . She looked for Joe, but she never matched him up with French, the guy in the papers."

"Whose idea was the adoption?"

"Hers. She fought with Denise about it. I heard. There was gossip, all right. And I knew what to do. You're right, my wife's still a maternity nurse. Elise would eat lunch at the restaurant where Dora worked. Dora had to work right up until the baby came. No money saved, Joe gone. My wife, she'd talk to Dora, make up stories. She was an adopted child, she'd say, or some such stuff, and she'd never ceased to bless the day when her poor unselfish mother gave her up for adoption, gave her all the advantages of family life.

"Dora didn't have many friends. My wife became her best friend, her prop to lean on. When it came time for the birth, it was my Elise who recommended a hospital, a doctor. Everything would be taken care of. And it was.

"There's always been a market for babies. The structure was all in place. My wife knew who to pay. It was a fine thing we did. Best thing I ever did. Dora would have given up the child anyway. Was it so wrong to grant Jeannine's wish? To save her marriage? To keep Fontenot's daughter Fontenot's daughter?''

Dora snored softly in her chair.

''What did you tell Joe?''

''Not a word. He thought the kid was his and Jeannine's, conceived right before he moved out. That's what she told him, that's what she told everybody who didn't know the truth. She lied about the kid's birthday. Aimee's younger than she thinks.

''Then after a while, Jeannine didn't want to see me anymore. That was hard. I suppose I reminded her that the baby wasn't her blood kin. She loved that baby more than she loved Joe, more than me. When Aimee was five, six years old, Jeannine asked me to stay away. I've hardly seen her since.''

''Does Jeannine know the child is Joe's?''

''Stay where you are.'' The knife glistened close to Dora's throat. ''I never told her. I think maybe she knows. It didn't make a difference. She wanted that baby. She loved that baby the minute she set eyes on it. You know, she never knew about Joe and prison. Used to make me laugh sometimes. There she was, so scared he'd find out her secret. And there he was, so scared she'd find out his.''

Where the hell were the police? ''Why frame Dora for killing Fontenot?''

''I didn't plan it that way. I was going to run away, lose Joe somehow. But then I saw her at that seminar and she was like a gift.''

''Even if she could be proved innocent, you thought she'd confess if you threatened to incriminate her daughter.''

''I never thought it would come to that. I never thought you'd start nosing around. It was an impulse, taking her knife. She set it down near me. I just touched it, to see what it felt like. And nobody was lookin'. So I slipped it

189

up inside my shirtsleeve, and it felt good and cold and hard. I thought, well, if she says anything about missing it, that's as far as I'll go. But she just locked the case real careful and never said a word. And Joe—Joe was so full of himself at the banquet, talking about his 'friend's' funeral. Just remindin' me that he knew about T-Bob. That knife started burning up my arm.

"We'd agreed to meet in here, while dessert was being served. So I could pay him. I was supposed to pay him for the rest of my life. Everybody was milling around by then. Lots of people drunk."

"You?"

"He was gonna ruin me, take everything away. After what I'd done for him, saving his only child—"

"That's one child who might have done better unsaved."

"Prison changed Joe. Made him hard and mean and narrow, always grabbin' after that time he lost. I didn't know he'd turn out like that. I had the child's best interest at heart. I want you to believe that. It was a good deed."

"It doesn't even the score. You killed two men."

"Two." Armand repeated the word softly.

Spraggue moved a step closer. "I know what Fontenot knew. About the body in the cemetery."

"I swear to you," Armand said. "I killed T-Bob in self-defense. He went crazy and killed a guard during that robbery. He planned to double-cross me, take the money—"

"It doesn't matter now. It may have mattered then, but not now."

"I was forced into doing what I did. There was no other choice I could have made."

"There's a choice now. Let me get Dora out of here. Before it's too late. What did you give her?"

"Stay where you are."

"Come on, Armand. If you were so innocent back then, why did you bilk Fontenot out of his share of the loot? Why'd you tell him T-Bob ran off with the money?"

"He would have had something on me the rest of my life if I'd told him I killed T-Bob. The way he was when he came out of that jail, he would have used it. Something happened to Joe in prison. It was a different man walked out."

Spraggue took two steps forward. Armand, now deep in the past, didn't seem to notice.

"Besides," he said faintly, "I got used to thinking of that money as mine. I opened my own restaurant, lived my dream. I never had that rich uncle, only the dream. I was settled. I paid my debt to Fontenot, with his daughter."

"Fontenot believed in your rich uncle?"

"Right up until they opened that tomb."

"Why not?" Spraggue said. One more step. "You were friends."

"Yeah, we were friends."

"He knew as soon as he saw the article in the newspaper?"

"He knew we'd planned to meet at the cemetery."

Another step. "Let me take Dora out of here. That's all I want."

"Stop!" Armand held the knife to Dora's chin, freezing Spraggue in his tracks.

"She's no good to you with a knife in her throat, Armand. Her death has to look like suicide or the confession won't stick, right?"

"She can stab herself." Armand's hand moved slowly. "In the gut, maybe. Like Joe. She will, if you come one step closer."

"It won't work, Armand. Very rare, a knife suicide. And they'll do an autopsy, find whatever you gave her, wonder why she took something first. And besides, there'll be a witness, won't there?"

That made him pause. His tongue flicked out and licked his lips again. "Yeah," he said. "I see. Now, listen to me. You don't want her cut right now, you walk over here real slow."

Where the hell was Rawlins?

"You figured out where she'd go to kill herself," Armand said softly. "You tried to stop her. She picked up a knife and—"

Armand's arm flew upward. He shouted, and Dora was out of the chair, a ribbon of red across her forearm where the knife had sliced a path. She was up, conscious, but too drugged to stand. She clung to Armand's neck, bowing him with her weight. His hand moved with the knife.

Spraggue was there, grabbing Dora by the shoulders, throwing her as far as he could, away from the knife. She fell like a dead weight, but he couldn't worry about her now. Armand had forgotten her and was coming for him.

Spraggue's hand searched the table behind him, found a pot lid, threw it in Armand's face. The man ducked but kept on coming, waving the knife before him.

Out of the corner of his eye, Spraggue could see Dora struggling to her feet. "Stay down," he hollered. "Get out."

Armand turned his head. Spraggue had the handle of a pot now. Hoping it was a huge skillet and not some tiny crêce pan, he aimed it at Armand's forearm.

The chef turned back, moved his arm, and scored a slice on Spraggue's wrist. Spraggue dropped the pan, but was able to put a table between himself and Armand.

Dora was hanging on to a red-checked tablecloth to keep herself upright, staggering toward Armand, not away. Her lips were moving, but Spraggue couldn't make out any words. She grabbed something off a table. It flashed in her hand.

Armand turned first one way, then the other. He decided on Dora. He could get her out of the way quickly, drugged and staggering as she was, then come back for Spraggue.

A slim metal rod hung overhead, chained to the ceiling, dangling heavy Calphalon pans. Spraggue clambered onto a tabletop, put one hand on either end of the rod and pulled, letting his weight bring the whole assembly down.

The clatter stopped Armand, but only for an instant.

Spraggue freed the rod, a shaft of steel six feet long. One end had the chain still attached. He jumped off the table. He couldn't see Dora.

The banner was white with bright red script. *Chicago Cutlery*. The upright cabinet had sliding glass doors. Locked doors. He swung the metal bar like a baseball bat. The glass cracked and shattered. He ran the bar around the frame, loosening jagged fragments, clearing space for his arm. He stuck one blade, Shakespearean dagger size, in his pocket and grabbed a longer knife by its dark wooden handle.

"Armand!" he yelled. "Dora!"

A clatter of pots and pans came from his left, two rows away. He vaulted over a table, pushed a cart aside.

Armand knelt over Dora, his upraised hand clutching the knife. Her hand gripped his forearm, pushing it back, but the look on her face said she couldn't keep up the battle much longer. Her eyes were open and unafraid.

Spraggue crooked his left arm around Armand's throat, pressed his blade against the man's back. "Drop it," he said.

The chef's knife fell to the ground and Spraggue kicked it away. It glittered on the carpet like a fallen branch from a silver tree.

"I'm taking Dora out of here," Spraggue said.

"I thought she was unconscious," Armand muttered. "I thought she was dead."

She lay huddled on the floor. Spraggue could hear her panting weakly. He couldn't see her face. Blood welled out of deep cuts on her forearms.

"I've got to get her to a hospital."

"Go ahead."

"The police will be here soon."

"I won't leave." Armand stared at the knife on the carpet, four feet away, out of reach. "It's over."

"That depends on you," Spraggue said.

Twenty-Four

The witchcraft shop lost a lot of magic in the daylight. The crowded shelves were less enticing through a film of dust, the gimcracks tawdry instead of bright. A fly buzzed Spraggue's ear as he stooped to pick up a blue plastic voodoo doll marked with darker blue arrows and circles. He wondered if the price included pins. If the place had been lit only by candles, he couldn't have read MADE IN TAIWAN on the tag.

Dressed in a bland skirt and blouse that could have outfitted any salesclerk, Sister Delores in the daytime wasn't half the treat she'd been at night either. Spraggue hoped his aunt would enjoy her "psychic reading" nonetheless. He thought she would. Rawlins was with her, and occasional explosions of laughter erupted from the back room.

He closed his eyes. The shop still smelled of potent magic.

"Your aunt, *monsieur*, she will be ready soon to leave for the airport?" Dora's voice startled him. She'd lost some of that fine-drawn look of the past week, but her voice was tight and quavery. She hadn't smiled since she'd woken up at the hospital, unsure of where she was, of what had happened. They'd hardly spoken since.

"As soon as Flowers comes, we'll leave. Don't worry." He replaced the voodoo doll on the counter and turned to investigate a bookshelf.

"*Monsieur*," Dora murmured. "I wanted to thank you."

"Look, you didn't kill Fontenot. The jury would have come to that conclusion if the police hadn't realized it before it got that far."

"No, not for that. I don't thank you for freeing me from jail. It sounds terrible, I know, but I wish to thank you for Paul Armand's death, for his silence."

Spraggue stared at the wooden floor. "You can thank me for his silence. I don't want credit for his death."

Rawlins had described the scene in the Imperial Orleans display room. Suicide by knife. Rare, but it happened. Spraggue didn't want to think about it. He was sure he would dream about it often, red splashed against the golden carpet.

"Can I ask you something?" Spraggue said to chase the memory away. "That night when you tried to sneak out of the hotel . . . ?"

"It must have been Armand. I got a phone call, a whispery voice, disguised. Someone said if I went to the Old Absinthe House I would learn something about my daughter."

Spraggue thought, if she'd gone out that night, she'd never have come back.

"Did the voice tell you to leave a note in your room?"

"Yes. Later, I ripped it up. I couldn't leave because you were there, and I didn't know whether to believe the voice."

"You recognized the voice when he called again?"

"Yes, and by then I knew he spoke the truth, because I had seen her for myself."

"You knew she was your daughter, right off, when she came to the hotel. How? She doesn't—"

"No," Dora said softly. "She doesn't look like me. But when I saw her standing in the light—my mother died when I was young. I haven't thought of her in years, but I could see her standing there, my mother. My daughter."

"Armand must have been watching the hotel. Or watching Aimee."

"He said she killed him. That she was my little girl and she killed him. I believed him. I shouldn't have, perhaps. But I didn't—I don't know her, and that man, the man my Jacques had become, I could believe any vile thing of that man."

"You haven't told her? Told Aimee?"

Dora's voice was a whisper. "I can't."

"Why?"

"Jeannine."

"What do you owe Jeannine?"

Dora shrugged. "She raised my child as her own. Think of it, *monsieur*. If your life was based on a lie, a lie you told once a long time ago, almost as much to yourself as to the rest of the world, would you want someone to come along and jerk the tablecloth and smash all the crystal?"

"Jeannine set too elaborate a table. She could have told Aimee she was adopted."

"How? With Joseph there?" Dora's hands moved over the shelves, touching, brushing, lifting, as if they had a will of their own. "I told myself once that it would be enough for me to know that somewhere in the world I had a child, to imagine that the child was happy."

"It's not enough?"

"Not today." She dropped a deck of Tarot cards, using their recovery as an excuse to duck her head and look away. "Today I want to make everything over in my life. I want to take that girl in my arms and say to her, anything I have is yours. Just let me make up to you the time I took away from you. And then, I realize that she doesn't know. For her everything is the same. She'll never know."

Dora placed the Tarot cards carefully back on the shelf,

lining them up with the edge, squaring the pack. Her hand shook. "In my head, I think that Jeannine had no right to make it as if I never existed. I think, in my head, it would be wrong for me to say a word. Aimee has a mother. Jeannine has a daughter. With a word, I could tear them apart. And my heart would like to say the word."

A floral-print tourist marched in the door and announced to her camera-toting companion that the place was just too precious. Spraggue searched for comforting words. None came. None adequate. He put his hand on Dora's shoulder.

"I'll wait outside," she said. "For the cab."

Damn all impossible choices, Spraggue thought. Where was Flowers anyway? Shouldn't he have picked up Pierce and the luggage at the hotel by now?

He picked a handful of colored gris-gris charms out of a basket. Blue, gold, white. Love. Money. Protection.

What was his hurry? No acting job to scramble back to. Nobody else's life to lead. His old actor's terror seized him, the feeling that somehow, without someone else to play, without a mask to slip over his real face, he would disappear.

No lover. No son, no daughter.

The cloying smell of aromatic herbs made him cough.

Aunt Mary and Rawlins emerged from the back room, with the sergeant beaming like a novice poker player trying to conceal a royal flush. Sister Del's melodious voice invited them to stop by again, any time.

"Your aunt has an aura of positive energy," Rawlins said to Spraggue.

"I could have told you that," Spraggue said.

"A lot you could have told me," Rawlins said.

"Your line was busy," Spraggue said. "Maybe I should have kept on trying, but I wasn't sure they'd be at the Imperial Orleans. I thought we'd have a better shot if you checked the other possibilities. I'm sorry."

"And I'm sorry for not gettin' there on the dot. That damned cabbie of yours—"

"Stop rehashing it," Mary said. "It all worked out fine." She tucked her hand into the crook of Rawlins' elbow. Her aura of positive energy had mussed a few of her red and silver curls and tangled them over her forehead.

"Sister Del spin you a good tale?" Spraggue asked. "Fame and fortune?"

"Romance," Rawlins said. "Definitely romance."

"Michael," Mary said, gazing straight at Rawlins though she spoke her nephew's name. "If you and Pierce can manage without me for a few days—"

"I can. I don't know about Pierce."

"I've never actually seen Mardi Gras," she said.

Rawlins' grin spread over his face and lit up his eyes. Magic.

Flowers pulled the cab halfway up onto the sidewalk and tooted the horn.